LOVE OR NOTHING

It seemed too good an opportunity to miss . . . Impoverished by her father's death, Kate Spenser has been forced to give up music lessons, despite her talent. So when the enigmatic pianist John Hawksley comes to stay with her wealthy neighbours, Kate cannot resist asking him to teach her. She was not to know Hawksley's abrupt manner would cause friction between them, nor that the manipulative Euphemia would set out to ensnare the one man who seemed resistant to her charms . . .

Books by Jasmina Svenne
in the Linford Romance Library:

AGAINST ALL ODDS
THE RECLUSE OF
LONGWOOD PRIORY
MOONLIGHT AND SHADOW
TO LOVE AGAIN
FORTUNES OF WAR

JASMINA SVENNE

LOVE
OR
NOTHING

Complete and Unabridged

C-1

LINFORD
Leicester

First published in Great Britain in 2011

First Linford Edition
published 2012

British Library CIP Data

Svenne, Jasmina M.
    Love or nothing.- -(Linford romance library)
    1. Love stories.
    2. Large type books.
    I. Title II. Series
    823.9′2–dc23

ISBN 978–1–4448–1074–5

Published by
F. A. Thorpe (Publishing)
Anstey, Leicestershire

Set by Words & Graphics Ltd.
Anstey, Leicestershire
Printed and bound in Great Britain by
T. J. International Ltd., Padstow, Cornwall

This book is printed on acid-free paper

1

Mrs Buckingham sighed, twisting the handle of her parasol one way, then the other. 'There you are, my dear. Is your mother not at home?'

'No, she went out half an hour ago. I'm sure she won't be long if you'd care to step into the parlour and wait.'

But Kate had already followed Mrs Buckingham's anxious glance at the other occupants of the landau, particularly the dignified, willowy figure seated beside her.

'What about the bishop, Mamma? We can't keep him waiting,' her older daughter interrupted, bestowing a serene smile down on Kate. 'I'm sure Miss Spenser is perfectly capable of passing on a message.'

Kate tried not to let her smile grow strained. She could feel the tension in the back of her neck from being forced to look up at the trio seated in the open carriage beneath a canopy of delicately frilled parasols.

There hadn't been time for Kate to snatch up her leghorn bonnet before the servant had informed her that Mrs Buckingham wished to speak to her or her mother at the gate. The message had surprised Kate. It was completely out of character for Mrs Buckingham not to step inside the cottage when she called. Now Kate thought she detected Euphemia Buckingham's hand in the matter. It was not so very long since the two young ladies had been Effie and Kitty to each other. But all that had changed.

'Yes, yes, to be sure.' Mrs Buckingham turned her ingratiating smile back towards Kate. 'Perhaps you have already heard that we are expecting guests at Fairfield Hall tomorrow?'

Neither Mrs Buckingham nor her daughters had talked of much else since their return from London. The whole village was buzzing, not least because

2

several cottagers' wives had been paid handsomely to go up to the hall to assist the servants.

'All manner of people are coming, even Mr Hawksley, the celebrated musician. I daresay you have heard of him?'

Kate assured her that she had and refrained from pointing out that all the newspapers from Fairfield Hall were passed on to her mother: She had seen John Hawksley's name mentioned several times in the London papers as a brilliant pianist and promising composer. She knew little else, except that he was reputedly very handsome and still quite young.

'Such an honour to be introduced to him at Bath last winter,' Mrs Buckingham murmured dreamily. 'Though I confess I was a little frightened of him at first. I do hope he won't find this little village of ours frightfully dull.'

'Mamma,' Orinda, her younger daughter, interrupted with an affectionate but exasperated smile. While Mrs Buckingham's eyes were averted, Kate took the opportunity to adjust her position so the August sunshine would not beat quite so mercilessly on her unprotected head. She stiffened as she met Euphemia's amused gaze. 'The invitation?' Orinda prompted.

Unlike her sister, Orinda took after her mother, being small and plump, without a single sharp corner in her whole body.

'Oh, yes, the invitation. You will come and dine with us the day after tomorrow, won't you? We're planning a little musical evening in Mr Hawksley's honour. You have no prior engagement, I hope?'

Kate managed to repress a wince. Nowadays, invitations were few and far between, and most had to be refused unless they were within walking distance or someone offered to make room for them in their carriage.

'No, we are free that evening.'

Euphemia ostentatiously consulted a tiny gold watch that hung at her waist, but her mother appeared not to notice.

Her eyes remained hovering on the house behind Kate.

'It must be dreadful being poor and having to live in such a pokey little place,' she said, peering at the two-storey, half-timbered house with leaded windows and a riot of native flowers in the garden. 'When I think of what your mother was born to, and that delightful house you used to live in . . . '

Kate swallowed a bitter lump of homesickness. Although they had lived in Fairfield Cottage for more than a year, she still missed her friends and the giddy social whirl of the county town, even if she was not sorry to get away from the riots about low wages, high prices and new machinery that had been rife in recent years.

'Fairfield Cottage is quite large enough for a small family,' she replied. 'We are both grateful to Mr Buckingham for agreeing to lease it to us.'

'Are you? Really?' Mrs Buckingham brightened considerably, if only for a second. 'Well, if you are comfortable, I suppose . . . but the windows are so tiny and I cannot think where you keep all your possessions.'

Only a tiny proportion of their belongings had been brought with them to Herefordshire, but Kate forbore to say so. If Mrs Buckingham discovered they had sold everything unnecessary to pay off Papa's debts, there would be no end of unwanted items from the hall. Anything she did send would have to be displayed prominently, otherwise the lady of the manor would wonder out loud what had become of her gifts. And to make room for them, something of sentimental value would have to be disposed of.

Kate had had one such experience in the first week after they took up residence in Fairfield Cottage. Not being entirely familiar with Mrs Buckingham's character at the time, she had inadvertently remarked that the thing she missed most about her present way of life was having no musical instrument on which to practise. The very next day, their dinner was disrupted by clattering wheels, thudding hooves and men's voices. Kate had flown to the window and was stunned to see what turned out to be Euphemia and Orinda's old nursery pianoforte roped securely in a cart.

Space had had to be made for the instrument and even now, every time Mrs Buckingham called on the Spensers, Kate was obliged to play something so their benefactress could bask in the sense of having done a good deed. The fact that the piano had suffered a great deal, initially at the hands of energetic, juvenile musicians, then by being shaken along rutted roads, completely escaped Mrs Buckingham, who had no ear for music, but thought she did. But even a badly tuned piano was better than none.

Euphemia flicked open her fan with a report like a pistol shot. Mrs Buckingham jumped visibly, shaking the entire carriage.

'We cannot tarry any longer, Mamma,' Euphemia said, blending sweetness with acid. 'Have you forgotten we are dining with the bishop?'

'No, child — that is, yes — you are right as always, my darling,' Mrs Buckingham stammered before turning back to Kate. 'You won't forget to tell your mother, will you?' she asked one last time, her eye falling on Kate's plain cotton gown. 'You do have something to wear on such a grand occasion, I suppose?'

'I'm sure I will find something.' Kate flushed nonetheless, aware of Euphemia's ironic glance. She could almost read the question in her eyes — *which one will it be, the white silk or the pale blue?*

'My daughters have such a quantity of clothes they never wear and . . . '

'I shall manage,' Kate interrupted firmly.

'Are you sure?' Euphemia cooed with the sweetest of smiles. 'I have a cream silk gown with pink rosebuds you could have.'

We are not reduced to that level yet,

Kate screamed inwardly. 'No, thank you. You are very generous, but I cannot accept.'

'Mamma, we really ought to go,' Orinda intervened.

And so at last, amid farewells and best wishes to be passed on to Kate's mother, the landau finally pulled away. Kate watched until it vanished behind the first bend in the road before she returned to the house.

It was deliciously cool inside after being exposed to the midday sun for so long. As always when she was angry or frustrated, Kate sat down at the piano. 'I'll never wear Effie Buckingham's cast-offs, never, never,' she muttered through gritted teeth.

And yet, a few years ago, both girls had delighted in trying on one another's gowns. But they had been equals then. Kate's mother and Mrs Buckingham had been childhood friends and were delighted to renew their acquaintance when they met by chance five years ago, while Kate and Euphemia had been enjoying their first season in London.

The two girls had got on well at the time, though with hindsight, Kate could see she had overlooked certain hints about Euphemia's character. She had seemed put out if Kate was the first to be asked to dance or her musical abilities were singled out for praise. And she had always made an effort to be particularly charming to any gentleman who spoke to Kate for any length of time, even if she made fun of him behind his back. But none of those things seemed terribly important at the time.

Then two years ago, when Kate was nineteen, her life changed suddenly and dramatically. Her father's death had been such a shock, she had not noticed until long afterwards that he had left his finances in deep disarray. It had taken her mother and the family lawyer many months of patient unravelling to uncover the extent of his debts.

'The fact is, Kate,' her mother told

them, 'we have been living well beyond our means for years. Your father was never much good with money, but he never wanted me to meddle, perhaps because he was ashamed of the straits he had gotten himself into.'

'Do we have anything left at all?'

Her mother smiled. 'It is not quite as bad as that. I still have the money that was settled on me when we married. He could not touch that, although he did hint once or twice . . . However, we should have enough to live on, once the house has been sold.'

In all their tribulations, Mrs Buckingham had never deserted them. She had married above her station, which perhaps explained why she often seemed intimidated by her husband and children, but nothing could quell her warm heart. She coaxed her husband into letting Fairfield Cottage to the Spensers and sent them fruit from the orchard or the odd pheasant, if her husband or son had a particularly good day's sport.

Even so, Kate had seen her mother cut corners so she could always put a decent meal on the table if they had guests and ensure her daughter had the minimum number of gowns so as not to excite comment. But they had slipped from cheerful extravagance to something like genteel poverty.

★   ★   ★

'You look beautiful,' Mrs Spenser assured her daughter affectionately.

Kate tugged a rebellious curl and smoothed her shimmering silk skirts. In truth, she was secretly quite pleased with her appearance. She had hesitated a good while between her two best dresses, the white being more virginal, whereas the blue matched her eyes. In the end, the latter won, for the simple reason that Mrs Buckingham had sent an apologetic note to say she could not send a carriage to fetch them after all and would they mind terribly having to walk? The road to the hall was pleasant enough, but Kate decided the blue gown would show the dust less than the white.

Nonetheless she paused on the threshold of the drawing room of Fairfield Hall, almost frightened at the prospect of such a grand party. She had to make a good impression. There were bound to be eligible men present, some of them perhaps rich enough to make her lack of a fortune no obstacle to marriage. Mrs Buckingham was a careful mother with an eye to her daughters' future. Orinda, it was true, was only eighteen, but Euphemia, like Kate, was twenty-one — and spinsterhood beckoned equally for both of them, the only difference being that Euphemia was cushioned by wealth.

It was not that Euphemia had ever lacked suitors. She had received two or three offers of marriage during her very first season in London, only none of the proposed matches was quite grand enough to suit her or her father.

Some of the company had already assembled in the drawing-room. Mr Buckingham remained aloof, but his wife received the Spensers warmly. Kate recognised some of those present, though she knew nobody well. She looked up as the door opened and her breath caught.

The man who had just entered was perhaps thirty years old and heart-stoppingly handsome, despite the absence of a smile in his eyes or on his lips. Amid all the finery, he distinguished himself with the simplicity of his apparel, his upright bearing and the steadiness of his gaze. Obviously he was someone important as Mrs Buckingham bustled towards him, clasping her hands to her breast to still her throbbing heart.

Kate was forced to admit Euphemia looked ravishing as always with her golden curls clustered around her oval face. All heads turned in her direction. Her new polonaise-style gown, obviously made according to the latest fashions, eclipsed Kate's gown completely. Perhaps that was why she made a point of slipping her arm through Kate's, as if she could not bear to be parted from her, and promised to introduce her to everyone. At such close proximity, Kate could not help being aware that most of the men, even those old enough to be her grandfather, were at least half in love with Euphemia. She drew tributes of smiles and glances wherever she went. All save one.

The handsome stranger bowed coolly towards her, as if merely from politeness. Euphemia, undeterred, bestowed her warmest smile on him. That told Kate more than enough. Euphemia was piqued by his indifference and, whoever he was, Kate knew that he was Euphemia's next intended victim.

'Mr Hawksley, I don't believe you have met my dear friend Miss Spenser,' she cooed. 'Miss Spenser is considered to be quite the finest musician in this neighbourhood.'

A sudden wave of shyness overwhelmed Kate. It would have been hard enough

15

talking to the handsome musician without this unexpected compliment, especially as she was certain Euphemia's praise was neither sincere nor disinterested.

'Indeed?' Mr Hawksley replied. 'I shall look forward to hearing you play.' Her awareness that he was only being polite made Kate squirm and she was almost relieved when Euphemia intervened. Almost, but not quite.

'You must not be so modest,' she laughed, tapping Kate with her fan. 'You know you are Mamma's favourite protégée.' Having thus established Kate's subservient position, she turned her attention entirely to the pianist.

On closer acquaintance, Mr Hawksley proved rather distant and monosyllabic. Euphemia flattered and flirted with him, but did not seem to make much headway. When she placed her hand on his sleeve and tilted her head to a bewitching angle to whisper some trifling secret to him, his lips barely twitched into a smile.

They were forced to separate when

dinner was announced. As usual, Kate found herself at the obscurer end of the table, struggling to keep up her end of a conversation about crop rotation, while irrepressible laughter further up the table repeatedly interrupted her train of thought.

Once back in the drawing room, to her surprise, Euphemia graciously drew her into her circle. However, since the conversation chiefly revolved around Parisian fashions, London entertainments and anecdotes about Bath, Kate was compelled to be silent for the most part, since all her information was out of date or gleaned from newspapers.

When the gentlemen, Mr Hawksley among them, joined them in the drawing room and Mrs Buckingham suggested it was time for a little music, Euphemia dropped her eyes modestly, fanned herself and murmured, 'Lah, Mamma, I don't know how I dare in such illustrious company.'

Without raising her drooping head, she lifted luminous eyes up at the musician, though he did not seem to have noticed her words or her glance.

'You've played to larger audiences before,' Mrs Buckingham remonstrated. 'I'm sure Mr Hawksley would not be unkind, would you, sir?'

The musician started at the sound of his name. He had, then, apparently been genuinely absorbed in his thoughts. 'I — no, of course not,' he said, gathering his wits. 'No man of sense would expect the same quality of music in a private home as at a professional concert.'

The slightest scowl produced two vertical lines above Euphemia's delicate nose. She had clearly hoped for something a little more flattering. She was soothed somewhat by the persuasions of her other admirers and closest friends, who perhaps hoped their turn would soon follow to try to make a good impression on Mr Hawksley and prove him wrong.

Euphemia spread out her gown in pretty folds, arranged the lace ruffles on her sleeves and smiled enchantingly at the gentleman who trimmed the wick of the candle for her, before she cast a sidelong look at Hawksley. Kate watched him too. She knew that Euphemia played and sang accurately, though without much expression, and that she was considered to be extremely accomplished.

'How well do you know Mr Hawksley?' Kate asked Orinda, who was sitting next to her. She thought she detected the slightest twitch of the musician's shoulders as Euphemia's top C came out rather shrilly. Kate herself was too much of a coward to sing in public, knowing that her voice was apt to betray her at critical moments.

'Not well, but you know how Mamma is when she takes a liking. She's even persuaded him to give us music lessons while he is here.'

Kate suppressed an upsurge of envy. If she dropped the slightest hint, she knew Mrs Buckingham would arrange for her to share her daughters' lessons, but Kate felt she had already accepted too many favours from her kind-hearted benefactress.

'Have you heard about his tragic past?' Orinda went on. 'Apparently his heart lies buried in his sweetheart's grave, no woman able to console him.'

Now Kate understood. It was the sort of challenge Euphemia could not possibly resist, although there could be no question of marriage between two people of such widely differing backgrounds. Kate couldn't help hoping Hawksley would remain indifferent. If he was still grieving, she hated the thought of him becoming Euphemia's plaything.

It was not until late that Kate's turn to play came. By then, most of the party had settled to tea, coffee and increasingly boisterous conversation. As she seated herself at the piano, she felt a twinge of sympathy for Euphemia. Perhaps her elaborate preparations were not affectation after all. She too was tempted to fidget far longer than was strictly necessary before beginning. Her hands felt clammy and her stomach knotted with dread. She would have to pay attention if she did not want to make a fool of herself in front of John Hawksley. But when she glanced at him, she was perversely disappointed to find he was deep in conversation with Mr Buckingham.

The opening chord was weak with half the notes missing. Kate forced herself to ignore her mistakes and gradually she eased into the sonata. The emotion of the music took hold of her and although she stumbled here and there, she managed to keep going until the end, despite the hum of conversation and peals of laughter all around her. One more piece and she would have done the bare minimum and could ask to be excused.

She chose not to play from sheet music. Once she had learnt a piece, her fingers seemed to develop a memory of their own, instinctively finding the right chords, arpeggios and intervals. But it was a risky strategy. If ever she started thinking too much or too little about what came next, she was liable to get lost and sometimes found it impossible to pick up the broken thread.

And that was precisely what happened when she chanced to look up towards the end of a minuet and found a pair of grey eyes watching her. At some point, John Hawksley had left his seat and wandered across to the window and now he was standing just feet away from her. In the second that she was not concentrating, her fingers missed their way.

Kate felt her face reddening as she groped for the melody with her right hand, but even that was beyond her. The correct keys seemed to slip out of her grasp. She jumped as a man's hand appeared from behind her and swept her fingers from the keyboard.

'Best leave it,' a deep, sonorous voice Kate recognised as Hawksley's said in her ear. 'Most of those present haven't been attending and won't know the difference whether you finish it or not.'

Kate was acutely aware of Hawksley's shadow interposing between her and the light. She was so mortified, she didn't know where to look. Even the worst musicians had managed to get to the end of their performance. To have made such a mess, and in front of a man she had hoped to impress.

'I can do better than this,' she pleaded, darting her eyes up so quickly, she only got the haziest impression of his face. She could still feel the touch of his hand, though now it was on top of the piano. A large hand with long fingers, nails cut ruthlessly short, and a mourning ring on the smallest finger.

'I daresay. You have a modicum of talent, but have been badly taught.'

'Mr Hawksley, you will play something for us now, won't you?' Never before had Kate been so glad to hear Euphemia's dulcet tones. She slid from the piano stool and let him take her place. She needed a dark corner in which to hide. Looking round, she spotted an empty seat beside her mother.

'Finished already, darling?' Mrs Spenser asked. 'You are a little flushed.'

'Can we go home soon, Mamma? I don't feel well.' Run away home and never come back, at least not until John Hawksley had departed, and everyone else who had witnessed her humiliation.

'Mr Hawksley is about to play, dear. You would not wish to miss that.'

'No, Mamma,' she replied dutifully.

There was worse humiliation in store. Mr Hawksley began to play exactly the same suite of dances she had botched so horribly. Kate felt her cheeks reddening behind her fan. She did not need this demonstration of how inadequate her performance had been.

The applause and praise afterwards was effusive and, Kate suspected, indiscriminate. It was balm of a sort to discover that Hawksley was right. No one seemed to have noticed that the same piece of music had been played twice in a row by different performers. She waited in agony for him to play the sonata she had attempted earlier. Instead he launched into a fiendishly difficult prelude and fugue.

If she was honest, she had to admit she was not sorry she had been forced to stay. She was glad she had heard Hawksley play at least once, though humiliation prevented her from enjoying the music as much as she would have done in different circumstances.

By having a quiet word with Mrs Buckingham, Mrs Spenser managed to borrow a carriage to take them home. Kate had hoped they might be allowed to slip away, but such a thing was unthinkable to Mrs Buckingham, who sympathised so sincerely about her supposed illness that Kate was forced to smile wanly at several other guests, assure them that she was sure she would be better by morning and thank them for their good wishes.

Perhaps, Kate thought, she could extend her illness for a few days. It would be the perfect excuse to avoid John Hawksley.

2

Kate tossed and turned all night. Between bouts of humiliation, she was haunted by other doubts. Would Mr Hawksley have commented on her performance if it had been totally without merit? Or had he merely been trying to console her? She could even see that he might have done her a favour by stopping her increasingly frantic efforts before her blundering became obvious to even the most unmusical person in the room.

When she came downstairs, she found her mother frowning over a note from the family lawyer, saying that he would call that morning. Given the circumstances, Kate felt she could not worry her mother by feigning illness and, after breakfast, took herself off for a walk so as not to be in the way.

The whole world looked lush and green, the result of frequent showers that swept down from the Black Mountains. But Kate scarcely saw the beauty that surrounded her. A lawyer's visit was never good news. Why should this be any exception? She must find some way of earning some money. She could not remain a burden on her mother forever, and the only alternative was a mercenary marriage. She was so preoccupied, she did not see the figure leaning on a stile until she was within a few feet of him. Her eyes flew upwards and met those of Mr John Hawksley.

'Ah, Miss Spenser, I trust you are feeling better this morning?'

'Yes, thank you,' Kate replied, suddenly feeling much worse. He, of all people, must know what ailed her. Gathering all her daring, she went on, 'May I ask you something?' Hawksley bowed his assent. 'Did — did you mean what you said last night about — '

'About your talents? Yes.' He stiffened, wary of what would come next. But she was committed now and had to proceed.

'I — I wondered whether you might be willing to give me a few lessons while you are in the county.' She scanned his face for a favourable reaction and found none. Her heart sank. Did he perhaps think she was presumptuous, making too much of his words? And how would she pay him? 'I am aware I played badly last night, but . . .'

'Well, at least that is something,' he remarked dryly. 'But you realise my time is precious and I charge accordingly, and frankly, I am not convinced the expense would be justified in your case. What do you intend to do with your accomplishment? Use it to snare a husband?'

Kate flushed, but this time in anger. He had no idea how hard her life was and how necessary were the stratagems he could afford to despise. 'No, that is not the reason at all,' she retorted. 'I want to be able to earn my own living to ease the burden on my mother, and I thought that . . . ' Her words trickled away under the influence of his grave look. There now, she had admitted how poor they were and alienated Mr Hawksley in one fell swoop.

'My dear child, it is hard enough for a man to make a living in this profession. The best you can hope for is to be a governess, a schoolmistress or perhaps a church organist. And I would venture to guess that your abilities are already more than adequate to fill any of those roles.'

His tone was not unkind, but still she found herself wishing the earth would swallow her up. He was clearly relegating her to the same status as every other schoolgirl in the country, so she was probably not as talented as she thought she was.

'I see,' she said. 'I am sorry for taking up so much of your valuable time.'

And with that, she fled. She

thought she heard him call her name, but she ignored it. Whatever he had to say, she did not want to hear it.

* * *

Her mother was remarkably cheerful when she got home. It seemed the news had not been bad after all, so Kate had humbled herself to no good purpose. Depressed, despite the beauty of the day, she opened the parlour window to let in the warm, scented air and turned to the cast-off piano.

She lost all track of time and was still at the instrument an hour later. She did not even notice the voices outside the window. The music she played soared, swept her to a different world, before setting her down again gently with the last dying note when a trilling laugh made her jump. The honeysuckle that trailed round the window framed Euphemia's face.

'Good morning,' Mrs Buckingham called, appearing suddenly beside her daughter. 'We came to pay a morning call, but did not dare knock for fear of disturbing you.'

Mrs Spenser, who had been writing a letter of business at her desk, promptly invited the whole party in. While the Spensers' sole maid was despatched to open the door, Kate rose from the piano stool, wiping her hands against her skirts.

'My dear,' Mrs Buckingham said, kissing her cheek in the familiar way Euphemia vainly tried to curb, 'it must be wonderful to have such talent.'

It was as well Mrs Buckingham went on chattering, because Kate, raising her eyes, met Mr Hawksley's level gaze. He shook hands with her, a brief, powerful squeeze that threatened to break her fingers.

Though the party from the hall was not large, there were barely enough seats for all and Hawksley elected to lean against the windowsill instead. Having nowhere else to sit, Kate sank onto the stool with her back to the piano, while the others exchanged the usual pleasantries about the weather and everyone's health.

'You will play something more for us, won't you?' Mrs Buckingham beamed at Kate, before explaining to Mr Hawksley, 'I was quite shocked to discover Miss Spenser had no instrument to practise on, but as you see, we remedied the situation.'

Self-consciously Kate chose the simplest piece in her repertoire, so as to avoid mistakes. Suddenly she became aware of all the imperfections of the piano she had grown used to. The clicking of one of the keys, the jangling of certain strings. Most of the keys rose sluggishly, instead of springing into place, so that half the repeated notes were lost. But at least Kate was used to the deficiencies of the piano.

She winced when, unwilling to be left out, Euphemia suggested a duet. The instrument had obviously deteriorated since she had last played it. Predictably Kate took the lower, less showy part, but the melody kept disappearing because Euphemia had to struggle with the piano. Kate saw her grow flushed with annoyance and was afraid Euphemia might lose her temper, something she tried to avoid in public. However, by the time they had struggled to the end, Euphemia had had a better idea.

She lifted wistful eyes and said, 'Oh dear, I'm afraid I do need Mr Hawksley's help. Perhaps when we get home you could show me where I went wrong?'

'Certainly.' Hawksley's tone was dry, but Kate knew Euphemia would feel encouraged. Now she would have the perfect excuse to claim his exclusive attention. What's more, he would have to replace Kate with the bass part. That meant sitting in close proximity, elbows brushing accidentally from time to time, her left hand coming perilously close to his right. It was only a matter of time before Euphemia triumphed.

★ ★ ★

Kate was reading in the parlour on the following Monday morning when the sound of voices attracted her attention. Setting down her book, she went to the parlour door. Her mother was standing in the narrow passage and through the open front door, Kate caught a glimpse of a respectable, if poorly dressed man. He was dusty from a long journey and was clutching a large bag of tools.

'There must be some mistake,' her mother was saying. Mrs Spenser turned towards her, a small frown puckering her forehead. 'This man says he has come to tune our piano,' she said, 'but I had not sent for him.'

The job needed to be done, but Kate knew her mother was thinking about the expense. The man was growing agitated too, sensing a wild goose chase. 'This is Fairfield Cottage? And you are Mrs Spenser?'

'Yes, but — are you sure you were not meant to go to Fairfield Hall?'

The man bristled. 'Are you telling me I cannot read?'

Kate drew closer to her mother to protect her.

'I didn't mean to imply . . . '

'Look, I've travelled all the way from Hereford, so I'd like to know — '

'So sorry I'm late. I had hoped to be here sooner to explain.' Mr Hawksley's voice made all three of them jump. 'I took the liberty of hiring this man,' he went on, directing his gaze at Mrs Spenser. 'If I am to teach Miss Spenser, I would far rather do so on a properly tuned instrument.'

'But I thought . . . ' Kate's voice trailed away.

'I am willing to waive my usual fees if Miss Spenser proves to be a conscientious pupil,' he continued, still primarily addressing Mrs Spenser as he guided her towards the parlour. 'However, I shall expect to be reimbursed for my time and trouble if she is rebellious or fails to progress as much as I expect.'

'That is very generous of you, sir, but we cannot take advantage of — '

'Nonsense. It will make a pleasant

change to teach someone with a true feeling for music.'

Mrs Spenser and Hawksley disappeared into the parlour. The instrument-maker threw Kate a curious look, but when she did not move, he followed the others. The outer door was still open and she moved to close it. Then, changing her mind, she wandered out into the garden, feeling dazed. Through the open parlour window she heard the man begin to work on the piano and then the voices of Mr Hawksley and her mother saying farewell. He nodded to Kate in passing and was moving away when she suddenly called out, 'Wait, sir.'

'What is it, child?'

The last word made her flush. She was not so very much younger than him. 'I — I just wanted to thank you.'

His sternly handsome face did not relax one jot. 'Let us lay our cards on the table,' he said. 'If you are serious about improving your technique, the next few weeks will be the hardest you have ever endured. I will not spare you in lessons and I will expect you to spend every free moment practising, since my stay here can be only of a short duration. So if you should think better of it, you had better do so now.'

'It is a little late for that, sir, now that you have told my mother you will teach me,' Kate bridled.

'Not at all. If you choose, I can give you perhaps one lesson a week, pat you on the head, tell you that you are a good girl and your mother need never know there was ever any talk of anything more.'

Kate felt dizzy. Somewhere at the back of her mind, she realised Hawksley had paid her a huge compliment. He was offering her something more than he did with his ordinary pupils. 'No,' she said. 'If we are to do this, I think we ought to do it properly. All or nothing.'

'Good.' He extended his hand and she allowed her fingers to be wrung in his firm grip. 'You can expect me

tomorrow morning directly after breakfast. Oh, and by the way, I expect you
to start practising as soon as the
instrument-maker has left.'

3

It was a subdued and white-faced Kate that awaited Hawksley the following morning. She had not slept well and could not stomach any breakfast. Even without Hawksley's parting injunction, she would have wished to practise as soon as possible.

The enormity of what she had undertaken had only just sunk in. She was going to submit her musical talents, such as they were, to the close scrutiny of a famous musician, and she was terrified of being found wanting.

'We had better begin with that minuet you played at the hall,' Hawksley announced without preamble on his arrival.

'Must we?' Kate had been hoping to ease into the lesson more gradually.

A brief smile flashed across his face and it struck her that she had never seen him smile before.

'It is like getting back on a horse after a fall,' he said. 'The sooner you do it, the better.'

Obediently Kate found the right sheet music. Her hands shook so badly, the pages rustled audibly as she settled them on the stand. If Hawksley noticed her nervousness, he made no comment on it. Instead he strolled across to the window.

'Begin whenever you are ready and play it through to the end,' he said over his shoulder. 'We will take it apart afterward.'

After a jerky, tentative opening, the music began to flow more evenly. The piano was much improved after the ministrations of the previous day, though it could never vie with the one at Fairfield Hall.

As she approached the phrase where she had lost her way at the hall, Kate grew more tense. As a result, she tripped over it again and only managed to keep going this time because she had the sheet music in front of her. Nevertheless she got to the end and that, she judged, was progress. But the silence that followed the last note unnerved her. She glanced over her shoulder. John Hawksley was still by the window, hands clasped behind his back. She had expected some critique, good, bad or indifferent. Instead, without turning, he said, 'Play the first page again. And this time do it with a little more conviction.'

Kate did her best. During the second phrase, she heard Hawksley cross the room and she sensed him looming behind her. She had not quite reached the bottom of the page when he stopped her. 'How many notes in that chord?' he asked, pointing.

'Four,' she replied.

'And how many did you play?' The question was so unexpected, Kate couldn't answer it honestly. 'Play the phrase leading up to it again.' She did so and heard a mirthless laugh behind her. 'Yes, you played them all this time,' he conceded, 'but in all your previous attempts, at least one of the middle notes was missing.'

Kate could not dispute that. Her last teacher had always said she played with more feeling than accuracy.

'This is by no means an isolated example, Miss Spenser,' he went on. 'I want you to go back to the beginning and play it at half-speed and listen to what you are doing.'

And so, line by line, phrase by phrase, at times even bar by bar, Hawksley took the minuet apart, sometimes making her repeat the same section over and over again. Kate submitted to his instructions, though she flinched at every sharp word. Praise was scant and never much more than 'better' or 'good'. But even that seemed sweet by comparison.

They lost track of time. In the end, Mrs Spenser had to interrupt them when lunch loomed and they were still hard at work. Hawksley exclaimed at how late it was and took the briefest of farewells before striding to the Hall.

Kate wriggled her shoulders, aware suddenly of how stiff they had grown.

'I hope he doesn't intend to work you so hard every day,' her mother remarked. Kate deemed it safer not to reply.

★ ★ ★

Initially, however, Mrs Spenser's hopes were fulfilled. On the next two days, Hawksley took care to spend no more than an hour at a time at Fairfield Cottage. The Spensers kept earlier hours than the Buckinghams and Hawksley had taken to rising early so he could take the lesson with her and still get back to the hall before breakfast at eleven o'clock.

On the third day, however, the lesson once again over ran its allotted span. Mrs Spenser had just remarked that it was past eleven o'clock when the door sprang open and Euphemia Buckingham bounded into the room.

'My dearest Kitty, I've come to invite you — good heavens, Mr Hawksley, I had no idea you were here.' Her simper, however, suggested otherwise.

'I assure you, the surprise is mutual,' he replied dryly. 'You were about to issue an invitation?'

'Yes, indeed. Thank you for reminding me.' She turned towards the others, having bestowed her prettiest smile on the gentleman. 'It's such a glorious day, Mamma gave us permission for an al fresco breakfast and we thought you might like to join us.'

It struck Kate that there was no reason for Euphemia to deliver the invitation in person. She could just as easily have sent a note with the coachman. Looking back, Kate realised it had been naïve to think Mr Hawksley's visits to Fairfield Cottage would go unnoticed. Indeed, she was surprised Euphemia had not already found a way to disrupt the lessons. She had never been one to tolerate rivals.

While Kate and her mother donned

their hats, the other two were left alone. The cottage was so small that Kate could hear Euphemia picking out tunes on the piano. She could picture the scene perfectly, Euphemia at the instrument, her head winsomely bent so she could dart occasional glances up at the tall man beside her.

Once they were all ready, Hawksley helped them clamber into the landau, before he took the empty place beside Kate, with their backs to the horses. Throughout the journey, she was conscious of his proximity. Their fingers touched when her hat ribbons flapped in his face and she raised her hand to brush them aside. To Kate's surprise, once they had disembarked, Euphemia slipped a hand through her arm and drew her on ahead, leaving Hawksley and Mrs Spenser to bring up the rear.

'Come, you must tell me,' Euphemia said, dropping her voice; as they strolled towards the summerhouse where the other guests were waiting. 'What has our morose Mr Hawksley been doing at Fairfield Cottage?'

'Much the same, I imagine, as he has been doing at Fairfield Hall,' Kate replied. 'Teaching music.'

Euphemia opened her eyes wide. 'It must be costing your mother a fearful amount of money,' she said. 'I know Papa was quite cross when Mamma invited him here.'

Kate deemed it safer to change the subject. 'I have benefited a great deal from Mr Hawksley's lessons,' she said, glancing over her shoulder to make sure he was out of earshot. 'But don't you find him just a little frightening?'

Euphemia burst out laughing. 'Frightening? Good heavens, no.'

'But he is such an exacting teacher.'

Euphemia looked genuinely startled. 'Are we both talking about the same man? Mr Hawksley spends all his time gazing out of the window and barely says a word to me.' She smiled smugly. 'I even overheard him telling Mamma that there was not much he could teach me.'

Bile stung Kate's throat. How could she trust Hawksley's judgement now? Did he really prefer Euphemia's playing, or did this reveal he was nothing more than a sycophant, praising Euphemia solely because of who she was, while venting his bad temper on Kate, knowing that she was in no position to complain? She had thought Hawksley respected her and treated her just like his other pupils. Once, at the end of a lesson, he had even remarked on her progress. Now she did not know what to think.

But Euphemia was not done yet. She leaned closer and whispered, 'To be honest, I fear poor Mr Hawksley is falling in love with me.'

* * *

The breakfast party seemed very loud to Kate. For the most part she felt confused and unable to follow what was going on around her. She hardly ate, but nobody seemed to notice.

48

There had been no time to ask why Euphemia believed Mr Hawksley was in love with her and as they sat at opposite ends of the breakfast table, it was impossible to make any observations. Euphemia was the centre of attention as always and flirted with her nearest neighbours, trying to make Hawksley jealous. Kate had seen her use the same trick often enough. Perhaps it was working because Hawksley was silent and brooding. That was the trouble with quiet men; it was so difficult to tell what they were thinking. But Kate also knew that it was quiet men who felt most intensely.

He became more animated when the conversation turned to Mozart. 'The man is a singular genius,' he said. 'Don't you agree, Miss Spenser?'

'I did not think myself important enough for my opinion to carry any weight,' she retorted. Kate could have bitten her own tongue when she saw surprise register in his eyes. What had induced her to say something like that?

49

Fortunately there was no time for him to reply. A wasp chose that moment to swoop perilously close to Euphemia. She screamed and instantly three gallant cavaliers flew to her rescue, armed only with napkins.

Once the meal was over — and that was not until well after midday — Kate found herself drawn unwillingly into a riotous game of blind man's buff. Glancing round during the game, she discovered Mr Hawksley sitting beneath a tree with her mother, watching her intently. Or perhaps watching Euphemia, who happened to be next to her at the time.

Kate did not know how long she could endure this enforced merriment. When the game broke down in chaos, someone proposed a row on the lake. Against her better judgement, Kate was persuaded to go too, though she had never much liked water.

If it had been a quiet party, she would have minded less. But Euphemia and her friends were in wild spirits, calling from boat to boat, laughing loudly, changing seats and making the boat rock so violently Kate was splashed more than once. She knew her pleas would have no effect, so she sat silently, hands clenched so tightly that her knuckles turned white, praying for it to be over soon.

Hawksley, at the opposite end of the same boat, was equally taciturn. Kate averted her face when she accidentally caught his eye.

'If you have no objection, I'd like to return to the shore.' His voice rang as clear as a bell, though he made no effort to raise it.

There were protests from the others, but they complied. Kate's breathing grew shallow. Would she be allowed to escape? At last with a rattle of oars and a thud against the post of the landing stage, they reached the bank. The boat rocked as Hawksley sprang ashore.

'Anyone care to join me?' he asked, his eyes flitting over the company. 'You look a little pale, Miss Spenser.'

Kate felt a sick sensation hover at the back of her throat. Did she want to be alone with him? 'Yes . . . I think . . . Perhaps the sun is too hot for me,' she murmured. Euphemia tried to laugh her out of it, but Kate scrambled to her feet, gathering her skirts in one hand. Hawksley clasped her fingers and, taking a deep breath, she jumped. The toe of her shoe came to rest against his. His waistcoat was only inches from her face. He did not release her hand directly and Kate realised her legs were shaking so badly they would barely support her.

'May I?' John Hawksley was offering her his arm and she was in no state to refuse. 'I trust you are in no danger of fainting?'

'N-no, I don't think so . . . ' His nearness had a disturbing effect on her. His scent enveloped her. Taking his arm, she became aware of his strength.

'I think I might join you after all,' Euphemia announced suddenly. 'Mr Hawksley is right, Kate. You do look ill.'

'I'm fine, really. There is no need to fuss.'

But there was no stopping Euphemia and where she led, others followed. The painter was made fast and the rest of the party disembarked. Kate had no doubt the other boats would soon follow suit.

Hawksley led her to a nearby bench. Some of the older members of the party had been sitting there, but at some point while the young people were on the water, their elders had decided it was growing too hot and had strolled back to the house.

Kate closed her eyes, but it only made her more conscious of the brooding figure beside her. The scene seemed to be imprinted on her inner eye — the lake fringed with trees, the boats full of brightly-coloured figures, parasols bobbing, hat ribbons dancing on the slightest of breezes.

She could not rest for long. Euphemia made such a fuss, Kate was forced to rally as quickly as possible. Soon they were trailing back towards the house to spend what was left of the day in the drawing room before everyone dispersed to dress for dinner. Kate's mother had spent the afternoon gossiping with Mrs Buckingham and had plenty of news to tell her as they strolled home.

'You're very quiet, Kate.'

'I have much to think about,' she replied. Then, remembering how much time her mother had spent with the musician, she added, 'What do you think of Mr Hawksley, Mamma?'

'He's very reserved,' Mrs Spenser said, brushing a fly off her sleeve, 'though he is perfectly agreeable when he unbends. I don't believe he is comfortable being dependent on the goodwill of others. It hurts his pride — and he has a good deal of that.'

'I am not sure he likes me very much.' Her mind kept returning to Euphemia's revelations. Perhaps if she confided in her mother? But Mrs Spenser laughed. 'What is so amusing?'

'Nothing. Well, simply that Mr Hawksley said something very similar this morning about you.'

Kate felt her cheeks crimson. She watched an orange butterfly meander through the long grass so she would not have to look at her mother as she asked the next question. 'What did you tell him?'

'I told him it was nonsense, of course, though I did point out that he was a little hard on you at times and perhaps he did not understand you.'

'And?' Kate was not at all sure she wanted to hear Mr Hawksley's reply.

'He said, 'I understand Miss Spenser better than she thinks. She is no more part of Miss Buckingham's frivolous social circle than I am'.'

★ ★ ★

Kate thought a good deal about those words. As a result, she half-expected to see some change in John Hawksley, though she was not sure what form it would take. However, when he arrived the following morning, he merely apologised for being quarter of an hour early. Kate had been awake since dawn, so there was nothing to prevent them from starting straightaway. She had expected some reference to the picnic. Instead Hawksley picked up exactly where they had left off the previous day.

'You have not practised since the last lesson,' was his only remark.

'No, I — I had no time.' She could have practised the previous evening, but had not been able to summon enough energy.

'All the mistakes I thought we had eradicated yesterday have crept back in,' he said. 'What was wrong with that bar?' He pointed to the music.

'My tempo was uneven.'

'And here?' He pointed again to another place on the sheet music.

'I missed a note in the middle of the chord?'

'No, the wrong chord altogether.'

Kate felt the sore festering deep

inside her. He would not have treated Euphemia in this way. Some of those mistakes were old and ingrained, but at least one was an accidental slip she had never made before.

'We shall start again,' Hawksley said, patience fraying in his voice. 'Play that phrase again with the fingering I taught you yesterday.'

Kate did as she was bid, but the ball of fury inside her was growing larger.

'Again . . . No. Try it at half speed . . . Again . . . Now faster. No, all the notes even, if it is not too much trouble . . . Better. Again.' His endless demands flowed one after the other and Kate lost count of the times she repeated those same two bars before Hawksley finally said, 'Now go back to the beginning of the line and add it on.'

Habit was too strong. She realised only when it was too late that she had slipped into using her own more awkward fingering.

'Does nothing I say stay in your head for more than two seconds?'

It was the final straw and Kate lost her temper. 'You have no right to treat me this way,' she cried, jumping to her feet. 'I may be poor, but I do not see why I should be treated with any less consideration than Miss Buckingham.'

He looked startled for a moment, then he flushed. Kate felt a twinge of fear for she could see anger reflected in his eyes too.

'Don't you, by Jove? Been comparing notes, have you? Has it ever occurred to you that I drive you so hard because I think you show promise, whereas Miss Buckingham is wasting my time and her own?'

Kate slumped back onto the piano stool in the face of this onslaught. She had always known that Euphemia's musical talents were limited, but no one had ever been so blunt about it in her hearing. Nay, most people applauded her efforts, some because of who her father was, others because they genuinely did not know any better.

'Do you have any idea how painful it

is for me to listen, day after day, to that beautiful instrument being mistreated in that manner? Or what a relief it is to come here, despite the quality of that object?' He flicked a disparaging finger at the piano. 'Despite the disadvantages you labour under, you produce a quality of sound far beyond Miss Buckingham's capabilities.'

Warm blood gushed into Kate's cheeks. Praise from those lips was so rare, she was utterly overwhelmed. She began a stammering apology, but he dismissed it with a wave.

'Let us waste no more time — God knows how long it will be before we are interrupted. And mind, do not let anything I said go to your head, or I'll take back every syllable.'

Kate fixed her attention on the keyboard, but she was aware that Hawksley was still agitated, though he tried to hide it. She could hear him breathing rapidly and as she practised the phrase over and over again, gradually blending it into the bars that preceded and followed it, he began pacing the room. He did not praise her when she had corrected the mistake, but went on to work on the next section that was giving her trouble. At last he said, 'I suppose we have time to try it once more from the beginning.'

Kate forced herself not to panic whenever she approached one of the pitfalls. She managed to reach the end without being stopped, then waited breathlessly for his verdict. It took him a long time to choose the right words.

'Better. Some of the expression has gone now that you are concentrating so hard on the technical difficulties, but that will right itself in time, provided you practise before our next lesson.' He turned aside to look for his hat.

'Sir?' Kate cleared her throat as she rose. 'I — I would like to apologise for my outburst.' She would not feel right until she had uttered those words.

Hawksley gave her a penetrating look, then sighed. 'No, you were right to complain. I do forget myself on occasions. I shall try to improve my manners in future, though it would be unwise of me to make any promises.'

'Then you will shake hands and say we are friends again?' Kate asked, extending her hand.

One of those rare smiles illuminated his face, like sunshine on an overcast day. He was so breathtakingly handsome at that moment, Kate felt it like an ache in the core of her soul. 'Friends,' he answered, clasping her hand.

4

There was no lesson on Sunday so, in addition to practising her repertoire, Kate started learning one of Hawksley's own compositions. She was in two minds whether to tell him or to practise it a little longer, but the decision was taken out of her hands. On Monday morning, Hawksley failed to arrive at his accustomed hour.

Kate went through her repertoire while she waited, but there was not even a note from the hall. It was only when Mrs Buckingham called at about noon that she discovered John Hawksley had gone out riding with the Miss Buckinghams and their friends. *So that is that*, Kate thought. Given time to work her charm, Euphemia had triumphed. It was, she was sure, no accident that no one had proposed lending her a horse so she might go with them.

Mrs Buckingham was still at Fairfield Cottage when Annie, the maid, announced that there was a messenger outside with an urgent letter. Kate half-rose before she realised the servant was addressing her mother.

'Were you expecting news?' Mrs Buckingham asked Kate when Mrs Spenser had gone.

'Oh . . . no . . . not really,' Kate stammered, caught off guard. Even if the letter was from Mr Hawksley concerning her, it was only proper that he should write to her mother. She changed the subject and they chattered amiably, but it was a long time before Mrs Spenser returned.

'This is bad news, I'm afraid,' she said. 'It seems my Aunt Margaret is dying and has asked to see me.'

Kate swallowed. She had not seen Aunt Margaret for several years, but had not forgotten the dread her forbidding personage inspired. Nevertheless, she assumed she would have to accompany her mother to Nottingham-shire and endure the lectures on how she never did anything right.

And perhaps it was better for her not to be forced to watch Euphemia torturing her latest victim. There had been talk of excursions and amateur concerts when Rafe Buckingham, the heir of Fairfield, arrived with his friends . . . oh, to exchange this liveliness for Aunt Margaret's deathbed.

'I'm certain Mr Buckingham will lend you the coach as far as Hereford,' Mrs Buckingham said.

'That is very generous,' Mrs Spenser said, glancing solemnly at her daughter. 'I only wish there was no need for Kate to accompany me.'

'Can you not leave her with me?' Mrs Buckingham leapt at the idea. 'It seems such a shame for her to miss all the fun. Of course, she will have to share a room with Euphemia — I'm afraid I haven't a single spare bed.'

'Oh, but I cannot impose upon you,' Kate protested.

'Nonsense. Your mother is my oldest friend. You will let Catherine stay with me, will you not?'

Kate wondered what Euphemia would have to say to this, but judging from her mother's expression, everything had already been settled.

★ ★ ★

In the event, Euphemia behaved extremely well, managing to make a little space for Kate's belongings in her cluttered, heavily scented bedroom. The whole thing had to be organised in a hurry since the next coach to Birmingham departed at dawn the following morning, forcing Mrs Spenser to spend the night at the coaching inn.

Kate was awake early. Too restless to sleep, she managed to dress and slip out of the room without waking Euphemia. Finding an unlocked door, she stepped out into the garden. The air was chilly. Kate shivered, but went on. Walking would warm her soon enough and it was better to be moving about than sitting in the drawing room, pretending to read and actually watching the hands of the clock edge forwards.

She thought she had the place to herself, but as she entered the lime tree avenue, she was startled by a figure at the far end. Gravel rattled underfoot as she came to a standstill. Her first instinct was to pull back, but she checked it. She would have to speak to Mr Hawksley sooner or later.

'I was sorry to hear about your aunt,' he said, approaching. Merely cold, conventional words. But there was nothing cold about his eyes. 'I am also sorry I did not manage to come to Fairfield Cottage or send word yesterday,' he went on. 'I was on my way there when I was waylaid and all but abducted. Miss Buckingham can be very persuasive when she chooses.'

'Indeed she can,' Kate agreed. There was something different about him, a radiance she was sure she would have noticed if it had been there earlier.

'I trust you did not waste too much

time waiting for me to arrive,' Mr Hawksley persisted.

'No, I did not waste my time.' Kate smiled. 'I practised until Mrs Buckingham called. I have been trying to play something new, although I am not certain that I'm doing it correctly.'

'You had better show me before you have time to develop any bad habits. I suppose it is still a little early for a lesson . . . ' He pulled out his watch as he spoke and frowned. 'Perhaps we should go for a walk instead?'

Kate assented, though the prospect of being alone with him frightened her a little. But once the ice was broken, she discovered her mother was right — Mr Hawksley could be an entertaining companion. He told her about his tour of Europe, the sights of Venice and Rome, the privilege of attending one of Mozart's concerts in Vienna and the giddying excitement of Paris.

They sauntered to the end of the drive and back. Kate was astonished at how quickly the time passed. They had almost reached the house when Mr Hawksley surprised her by asking, 'Are you hungry?'

'A little.' She was famished, but she didn't like to say so. 'But breakfast won't be for hours yet.'

'I have an idea.' He pushed open the gate into the orchard. 'What would your highness like — apples, pears, peaches, plums, cherries?'

Kate smiled back, but she could hardly believe this was the same man she had almost feared. 'Oh, fie, sir! I fear you were a wicked youth and received more than one hiding for such thievish tricks.'

'True, but I lived to tell the tale, and I am willing to risk my neck again, if you'll conspire with me to dispose of the stolen goods.'

With that he plucked an apple from the nearest tree, rubbed it clean on his sleeve and offered it to her. Kate laughed and sank her teeth into the firm, juicy flesh. He picked another and they munched companionably.

'Do you think it is still too early for a lesson?' he asked when they had finally finished.

'Well, perhaps if you promise not to shout, we won't disturb anyone.'

'You minx! I'll teach you to respect your elders,' Hawksley retorted, laughing lightly. 'Come on.'

He set off at such a rapid pace, Kate had to trot to keep up until he noticed how breathless she was growing and moderated his pace. All too soon she was seated at the piano. The first notes seemed very loud, and playing on a strange instrument always took a little getting used to. Hawksley made allowances for this, permitting Kate to play each piece twice before commenting on her performance.

The lesson went better than usual. At one point Kate suspected Hawksley either overlooked one of her mistakes, or decided to ignore it. Throughout, she could not help but be aware of his whereabouts, sometimes standing close behind her, occasionally wandering away a few steps before coming back. There was a restlessness about him, like the coiled energy of a snake about to spring.

It was not till the last piece that he interrupted her. 'No, no, not that way. Here, let me show you.'

Before she could move, he had knelt on the stool with one knee, pinning her to her seat by her skirts. She could feel his leg pressed alongside her thigh and his arms almost encircled her as he placed his hands on the keyboard. She barely had time to draw her hands back into her lap. She hardly dared breathe. He was so close, his chest against her back, his arms lightly touching hers. She felt his warm breath waft through her hair. His scent made her dizzy and suddenly she knew. She was in love with John Hawksley and she wanted this moment to last forever.

The ripple of notes he coaxed out of the piano made her heart contract, then expand. Instead of stopping at the end of the phrase, he went on to the bottom of the page. Kate didn't dare move for fear of breaking the spell or betraying her emotions. His cheek, his lips were so close to hers. He would only have to lean a little closer to . . .

He straightened up, but remained half-kneeling on the stool. A shiver of electricity ran through her as his long-fingered hands settled lightly on her shoulders, thumbs resting either side of her spine at the base of her neck. 'Now let's see whether you were paying attention or daydreaming,' he said.

Kate flushed. Had he sensed something? She was achingly aware of his hands on her shoulders, his leg pressed against hers. If he had been conscious of these things, he would have drawn away. No, he scarcely knew she existed — he was thinking of somebody else.

Kate poured her pain into the music. It came out far better than she had expected. One of his hands lifted. Silently he leaned forward to flick the page over and, obeying his unspoken command, Kate went on without pause to the end of the piece.

'Good,' he said. 'A marked improvement.' His voice was muffled, and yet each syllable ruffled her hair. A tremor ran across her skin, as if every inch of it was alive. She could feel his eyes on the back of her neck and yet she did not dare turn round. She almost cried out as he drew away from her.

'You had better show me what else you have done,' he said. His voice had suddenly grown curt again and he moved over to the window for the first time that morning.

Kate told herself there was nothing unusual in his action or his change of mood, but she felt bereft. In the time it took to find the music, she struggled to regain her composure. She couldn't think about that revelation now. It had to wait until she was alone.

She threw one look at John Hawksley before she began. He was standing with his shoulder leaning against the window frame, his handsome face in profile and his arms folded across his breast. She barely had time to notice his compressed lips and no chance to wonder what his expression meant.

She had only learnt the first movement of the sonata. At the opening phrase, she heard him stir. She was aware she played better than usual. Perhaps that was what unrequited love did, she thought forlornly. She never lost consciousness of the dark figure on the edge of her vision. It was only after she stopped that she realised how still the house was. The rustling of her gown as she twisted her body towards him seemed loud by contrast.

At some point during the sonata, Hawksley had turned his back on her completely and dropped his arms. She could see his hands gripping the windowsill. Without warning, he jerked into motion. But instead of coming towards her, he strode to the nearest door. Kate heard swift steps, then the outer door opened and shut.

She let instinct guide her. Not even

stopping to close the lid of the piano, she hurried after him. He had already put half the width of the lawn between him and the house, but Kate did not care. Impetuously, she ran after him, oblivious to the fact she was being watched from an upper window.

Her footsteps were muffled by the grass. He did not seem to hear her. She caught hold of his arm for support, as well as to detain him, and panted, 'What is it? Have I done something wrong?'

And then she saw his face, the glitter of unshed tears behind his usually cold eyes. She dropped her hand in shock and staggered back a step.

'I am so sorry. I should not intrude.' And she turned to leave.

'No, don't go. Stay with me . . . '

His voice was so hoarse she scarcely recognised it. 'Of course I'll stay, if you want me to,' she whispered. His fingers clutched hers. He averted his face and she let him lead her forward until they reached the lichen-grown steps down to the next tier of the garden. There he stopped, staring at the blue ridge of hills in the distance.

'I was engaged once, a long time ago,' he said brokenly. 'She died a week before we were to be married. I had not realised she was so ill. I was away, teaching and composing and giving concerts, so I could earn a little more money. She didn't want me to be worried and so she asked her family not to send for me, but they grew frightened at her rapid decline. I wanted to marry her on her deathbed but by the time the parson came, she was unconscious.' His voice had grown quieter and yet each syllable was crystal clear. 'She died in my arms.'

Kate laid her hand on his shoulder. 'I am certain that was what she would have wanted,' she murmured. 'And it sounds as if it were a peaceful death.'

'It was, at least at the end, when she stopped fighting it. I did not know until afterwards how she — ' And there it was, the unmistakable catch in his voice. Kate did not press to ask any more. He should tell her only as much as he chose to.

'They say she was an inspiration, the way she was determined to wring every last ounce of enjoyment out of life. She fought to ignore her symptoms, to continue with her preparations for the wedding. If it were possible to overcome consumption by willpower alone, she would have done it. If her family had sent for me sooner, I might have drawn courage from her example. I don't blame them — I never have, for they meant well. But she was so broken and faded by the time I finally arrived, even though she tried to smile, despite that terrible cough . . .' His voice faded to nothing.

The silence stretched to infinity while Kate listened to the wind swish the grass and rustle in the trees. Somewhere far, far away, she heard a thrush's warbling song.

'I wrote that sonata for her. She asked me to play it for her one last time and though I managed to the end, I have been unable to play it again since.'

'I'm so sorry. I did not know.'

'How could you? I have never told anyone. It came as a shock . . . '

'Shh, I understand. You need not say any more.'

He bowed his head and looked at their clasped hands, as if realising for the first time what he was holding. Unwillingly he released his grip.

'I think I should like to be alone now,' he said.

'Of course.' Kate turned back towards the house. Halfway across the lawn, she turned and watched him go down the steps towards the lake, unaware that jealous eyes watched her too.

*　*　*

It was outrageous! Impossible. The sight of that pair together gave Euphemia a pang she mistook for unrequited love rather than hurt pride. Not only did she want the glory of capturing an unassailable heart, but she did not want her poorer, plainer friend to snatch victory from her.

She looked at herself in the mirror as her maid helped her dress, but she could not fault her face or her figure. She was taller than Kate; her hair was fairer, her features more regular. She wore fashionable clothes and, unlike Kate, who could sit silent for an hour at a time, she was always lively company. What more could a man want?

What stung her pride the most, however, was that she had known Mr Hawksley first. She trawled her memory, but could not find a single instance where a gentleman had looked twice at Kitty Spenser after being introduced to herself first.

Well — there were ways and means. She had discouraged other suitors of Kate in the past by studying their characters and playing on their weaknesses. One thought Kate too grave, so she laughed at his dull, repetitive jokes. Another admired Kate's scholarship, so

Euphemia pretended to be an ardent seeker of knowledge whose education had been shamefully neglected, even though she had sometimes been bored to tears by the man's prosing.

If she could find a chink in Hawksley's armour, she knew she could feign sympathy while administering poison, drop by drop, until he could no longer bear to be in the same room as Kate Spenser.

5

Days passed and Kate found her friendship with Hawksley was on an easier footing, at least externally. She had to watch every step so as not to betray her feelings, but he was gentler and praised her more often, and sometimes she even fooled herself that in time he would grow fond of her. But then, inevitably Euphemia would glide up and find some way of interrupting their tête-à-tête.

There was no repetition of the frivolity in the orchard, nor did they exchange any more confidences. By mutual unspoken consent, they avoided the sonata that evoked memories of his dead bride. Kate resolved not to play it until she returned home, and only then if she was sure there was no chance that Hawksley might call. He must be the one to broach the subject, if it was to be broached at all.

Much of Kate's time was spent strolling about the garden or the surrounding countryside, listening to Mrs Buckingham's tales of her youth, riding, calling on neighbours or shopping expeditions to Hereford. Being at the Hall meant she had to share the piano and Mr Hawksley's attention with the Buckingham sisters, and Euphemia had grown very diligent of late.

A letter arrived from Kate's mother, saying her aunt seemed near her end and so she would stay there for the present.

About ten days after Mrs Spenser's departure, Kate was returning from a walk with Mr Hawksley and the Buckingham sisters when they were startled by thundering hooves. Kate glanced over her shoulder, but the lane was winding and nothing could be seen.

'It sounds like a runaway carriage,' Hawksley said, pulling Euphemia, who was leaning on his arm, towards the nearest meadow.

Euphemia uttered a cry of horror and

clung closer to him, though craning her head around to see. Hawksley bundled her over the stile, but there was no time for the others to follow.

Side by side, one slightly ahead of the other, two phaetons hurtled round the bend in the road. Kate formed an instant picture of a tall, arrogant figure standing on the leading phaeton, feet planted wide apart and whip in hand.

If it had been a single carriage, there would have been room for Kate and Orinda on the grassy verge between the road and the drainage ditch. As it was, it was a miracle the second vehicle had not already toppled into the ditch, its wheels were so close to the edge. There was no time for thought or calculation. Tugging Orinda's arm, Kate dragged her into the ditch.

It was steeper than Kate had anticipated, overgrown as it was with cow parsley. Her feet slithered, although after a recent dry spell, the bottom of the ditch was dry. Orinda's arm slipped from her grasp. Kate fought to keep her footing, but she overbalanced and fell, twisting one foot beneath her with a wrench that made her cry out, just as the first phaeton thundered by, swaying dangerously.

Dust smothered her. Kate curled up in the bottom of the ditch, fighting for breath and trying to ignore the throbbing of her left foot. More hooves, more wheels, more dust, this time right along the verge on which she had been standing a moment previously.

She could hear hooves receding, Euphemia's shrieks, Orinda's hysterical laughter. Then everyone talking at once. John Hawksley sounded angry and there was another man's voice, lighter, more apologetic in tone.

Kate raised her head. Euphemia was clinging to Hawksley's arm while Orinda was scrambling out of the ditch unaided. Beyond them, she could see the back wheels of the second phaeton and a stranger approaching.

'I do not care for your feeble

apologies,' Hawksley was shouting. 'There is no excuse for such reckless-ness. What if a child had chanced to be in your way?' His head twisted over his shoulder as Orinda snatched his arm. 'Where is Miss Spenser?'

'I am here,' Kate called, but as she tried to rise, a sharp spasm made her cry out and her foot gave way beneath her.

She heard a flurry and a thud and suddenly found Mr Hawksley was in the ditch beside her, his earlier angry flush replaced by a deathly pallor. His arm was already around her waist, supporting her, as he said, 'You are injured.'

'It is nothing. I landed badly and wrenched my ankle, is all.'

Hawksley gathered her up in his arms, despite the narrowness of the ditch. The movement brought fresh pain. She gasped and clung tighter round his neck. She could feel his rapid breath on her cheek.

'Let me help, sir.' The stranger

stooped at the edge of the ditch and Kate looked up into an open, boyish face, wearing such a concerned expression, she almost felt sorry for him. 'You had better pass her to me,' he urged, holding out his arms. 'You will not be able to clamber out like that.'

Hawksley gave him a black look. Kate sensed that if he had had a choice, he would have dispensed with his assistance.

'You had better do what this *gentleman* says, Miss Spenser.' He spat out the word gentleman as if it was an insult.

'Sir, you cannot be more sorry than I about this incident.'

Kate found herself being transferred from one pair of arms to the other. The pain was making her nauseous. The stranger carried her over to the stile and Mr Hawksley, kneeling before her, carefully removed her shoe and began gently probing her injured foot.

'I do not think anything is broken,' he said, throwing another reproachful look at the stranger. 'But we had best call a surgeon to look at it.' He whipped off his neckcloth to bandage her foot. Another surge of pain brought Kate to the brink of fainting and she closed her eyes.

'There is nothing for it. I had better take her in my phaeton,' the stranger said. 'But you will have to give me directions. I was on my way to Fairfield Hall, if that's of any use.'

Both sisters exclaimed simultaneously. 'But that's where we live.'

'You must be Rafe's friend,' Euphemia added.

Kate realised the other carriage was nowhere in sight. Rafe Buckingham evidently had not noticed them in his determination to win the race.

'Frederick Clinton, at your service.' The stranger bowed gallantly.

His gaze moved from face to face, stopping at Euphemia. She dropped her eyes coyly. But it was Orinda who made the introductions, determined not to be overlooked because she was the youngest. Both sisters admired the phaeton and Clinton visibly relaxed at their warm welcome, while Hawksley took advantage of their preoccupation to scoop Kate up again.

'How far is it to Fairfield Hall?' Clinton asked.

'Half a mile, no more. I am certain I can carry Miss Spenser that far.'

'Oh, but, sir, there is really no need, not when I have my phaeton at your disposal. It is the least I can do to make amends.'

'Thank you, I have seen an example of your driving and would prefer not to risk the life of a lady who has been entrusted to my care.'

'You do me an injustice, sir. I am not always so reckless — my own mother drives out with me and she is a confirmed invalid.' Clinton appealed to Kate directly. 'Upon my honour, I shall go no faster than a walking pace.'

Kate was not overly keen to be hoisted into the ridiculously high seat of the phaeton in the company of a young man she did not know. She was slim and not very tall, and it was a subversive pleasure to be held in Mr Hawksley's arms, but she knew she would soon grow too heavy for him.

'Perhaps it would be better to accept Mr Clinton's offer,' she suggested. 'I should not wish to be a burden.'

'You are not a burden,' Hawksley insisted.

'It would ease my conscience . . . '

Hawksley glanced down at her face. His throat looked vulnerable and unprotected without his cravat. 'Very well,' he grunted.

With some difficulty Kate was lifted into the phaeton, watched enviously by the two sisters. They had not yet set off when Orinda spotted her brother returning. After greetings and explanations, it was decided that Rafe would go on ahead with Orinda to give an account of what had happened, while the others followed at their own pace.

Clinton was as good as his word. His horses were restive and ready for another run, but he held them in check.

Even so, it was inevitable that they should outstrip the pedestrians. Kate clung to the seat and glanced back over her shoulder.

'I assure you, Miss Spenser, you are perfectly safe with me,' Clinton said, noticing the look. 'Even if I were the most foolhardy man alive, I would think twice about crossing your fierce guardian. I have no doubt he would put a bullet through my brain if I let any harm befall you.'

'Oh, I am certain Mr Hawksley did not mean to — ' and then Kate realised he was teasing her. 'You are a wicked, unprincipled villain and I do not believe I ought to say another word to you,' she said, not hiding the smile in her eyes and voice.

Nevertheless, she felt disloyal, laughing at Clinton's jokes. She could not help remembering the sensation of being pressed against Hawksley's chest, or the touch of his hands on her injured foot. She shivered.

'You are not cold, are you?'

'No. I just — ' She stopped herself. To say anything more would be to reproach Frederick Clinton and he had been an amiable companion so far.

'Ah, you were thinking about the accident,' he said. 'Hawksley is right. There's no excuse for such behaviour, but you know how young men are, challenging each other to do mad things, and what with the brisk wind and the roads so empty — and Buckingham swore it would be perfectly safe.' He grinned ruefully. 'I suppose I'll have to pay up too, since he appears to have proved the superiority of his beasts. Or are you going to scold me for being a sad dog and gambling away my patrimony?'

'I am afraid I do not know you well enough to presume to scold you,' Kate replied primly.

Those were the last minutes of relative peace she was to enjoy for the rest of the day. Orinda's breathless tale roused the whole household and Mrs Buckingham was waiting on the threshold when

Frederick Clinton's phaeton drew up in front of the house.

Kate was carried to the drawing-room sofa. Clinton repeated the story with a good deal of humour, taking all the blame on himself. This, Kate judged, probably suited Rafe Buckingham admirably. Perhaps that was why the two young men were friends — Kate had never once heard Rafe admit he was to blame for anything.

She knew it had been Mrs Buckingham's dream, when the two families first became close, that Kate would marry her son, but there was never any chance of that. Rafe had always looked down on her as a companion of his silly little sisters and Kate had never been impressed by his swagger.

When the surgeon arrived, he not only put a more professional bandage on her foot, but insisted on letting some blood as a precaution and forbade her from placing any weight on her foot until further notice.

Hardly anybody noticed John Hawksley

follow Euphemia into the drawing room, nor the look of relief and pleasure that crossed his face when he caught sight of Kate. But it was quickly replaced by two vertical furrows just above his nose when he saw Clinton by her side.

As the afternoon progressed, the frown grew more pronounced and Hawksley's answers became shorter and blunter. Kate noticed that something was troubling him, but he kept to the far end of the room so she could not discreetly ask what was wrong. When the time came to dress for dinner, Clinton insisted on carrying Kate upstairs, despite Euphemia's hint that one of the footmen could do it.

As soon as the bedroom door was shut, Euphemia remarked, 'Perhaps you would prefer a quiet evening upstairs after your ordeal.' The trace of mockery in her tone implied she thought it a fuss about nothing.

Kate hesitated. On the one hand, she hated being treated like an invalid by the company; on the other, the prospect of an evening alone while the others were enjoying themselves was not appealing.

'Perhaps that would be best,' she said slowly, not wishing to impose.

'You've made the right decision.' But Euphemia's smile told Kate she had made a terrible mistake.

* * *

It was the longest evening Kate had ever passed. Euphemia lent her a novel, but she could not concentrate. First there were numerous footsteps, doors opening and closing, voices meeting on the stairs. She could hear snatches of conversation, laughter, music. Frederick Clinton's voice in particular invoked gales of laughter, and there was no mistaking Hawksley's exquisite playing. She could not help wondering if anyone missed her at all.

Only Mrs Buckingham had come to commiserate with her. Her sympathy almost made Kate cry, but she put on a cheerful face so her hostess would not feel worse. Tomorrow she would have to write to her mother, making light of her injury, to prevent her from being upset by a more excitable missive from Mrs Buckingham. She retired to bed earlier than usual, but pain kept her awake long after Euphemia had come somewhat noisily to bed.

Nevertheless, she rose early. She wanted to avoid a repetition of the previous night by being downstairs before anyone could stop her. She had second thoughts almost as soon as she lowered herself gingerly out of bed. She could only take one step at a time, clinging to the railing with both hands because she dreaded taking her full weight on her injured foot. She had not yet reached the stairs when she heard a door open behind her.

'Ka — Miss Spenser, you must let me help you.'

She glanced back. It was John Hawksley. Pinching her lips, Kate limped another step. 'Thank you, but I would rather be independent.'

'I do not wish for you to make your injury worse. At least lean upon me.'

He adapted his pace to hers, but at the head of the stairs, seeing her white face, he overruled her and gathered her up in his arms. It was incredibly tempting to nestle against him. He seemed so large, so warm, so reassuringly strong. Kate's heart contracted at the tender gleam in his eye.

'Now,' he said, placing her on the sofa, 'I forbid you to move.'

Kate had no intention of disobeying. Hawksley sat down at the piano and played softly so that by the time the others began to drift downstairs, Kate was almost asleep, still dwelling on the sensation of being held by the man she now knew she loved.

As soon as he entered, Frederick Clinton resumed his seat beside the sofa and asked after her health. 'I did not sleep a wink all night,' he confessed, 'for being tormented by guilt and the memory of your eyes.'

'I cannot believe that for a second,' Kate laughed.

She did not notice Hawksley frown and close the piano abruptly.

'Such a handsome couple, don't you think?' Euphemia Buckingham's voice roused him from his brooding.

'Which couple would that be?' he asked, hoping she had not noticed where his eyes had been directed.

'Why, Miss Spenser and Mr Clinton, of course,' his tormentor replied with a laugh. 'Kate cannot afford to marry a poor man and I cannot think of a more perfect match.'

★ ★ ★

It took two weeks for Kate's ankle to recover fully, though she could hobble short distances within days of her accident. But the time passed much more quickly and pleasantly than she had expected. Whenever he was not out shooting with Rafe, Frederick Clinton spent his time entertaining the company. He amused Kate with his stories, invented silly games with Orinda, read sentimental verse with Euphemia and flirted with all three.

The only fly in the ointment was John Hawksley. Kate couldn't help noticing his moods had grown darker. Nor had he got over his initial dislike of Clinton. The younger man chose to ignore most of the acidic remarks Hawksley made in his hearing, but Kate sensed a smouldering resentment that his attempts to befriend the musician had been repeatedly rebuffed.

So she was disappointed, but not surprised, when Hawksley refused to come with them on her first long walk since her accident.

'What glorious weather,' Kate remarked when they returned. Her cheeks were stinging from the fresh breeze and her ankle throbbed, but it seemed a small price to pay. She felt as if she had been pining for air for weeks.

'I always find it is the company that

makes an expedition pleasurable.' Clinton smiled.

'Indeed,' Kate replied, but looked to another. 'I'm sorry you will not come with us, Mr Hawksley.'

The musician had risen from the piano stool at their noisy entrance and did not lift his head as he gathered his scattered sheets of paper.

'I work better when the house is quiet,' he replied somewhat gruffly. 'Some of us have a living to earn.'

Kate felt the implied reproach. In barely more than a week, the Buckinghams were to host a concert at which she was supposed to play, amongst others. But with one thing and another, she had not had much time to practise recently and Kate knew she was under-prepared.

'Have you been composing something new, sir?' Euphemia exclaimed, gliding across to them. 'Won't you play it for us?'

'It is not yet complete.'

'I'm not surprised you have been

inspired,' Clinton said, seating himself beside Kate on the sofa. He let his gaze glide round the room to include all three young women. 'The presence of so much beauty must make composition easy.'

'Perhaps you ought to try it,' Hawksley replied dryly. He glanced at the sheaf of papers in his hands. Most were spattered with ink or had whole lines scratched out.

'But you must have a muse, sir,' Clinton persisted.

'Fie, sir, you shouldn't ask such things,' Euphemia giggled, tapping him with her fan. Kate choked down the urge to slap the coy smile from her face.

'If you must know, I am writing a sonata for a fellow pianist,' Hawksley said in chilling tones.

'How very prosaic.' Clinton made a face. 'I much prefer my explanation.'

'Ah, but you, sir, are an incurable romantic,' Euphemia said.

Kate found herself watching Hawksley's grim expression. Could he be jealous? Euphemia and Orinda constantly vied for Clinton's attention and, under that hard and cold exterior, Kate knew Hawksley was truly vulnerable.

Hastily she changed the subject to more general topics. Orinda seconded her efforts, clearly annoyed that her sister was monopolising Frederick Clinton's attention. But Hawksley remained sunk in gloom and when Kate attempted to address him directly, he replied only in curt monosyllables.

In the end she could not help asking, 'Have I done something to offend you, sir?' She thought he would smile and reassure her, but his frown only deepened. 'I should apologise profusely, if you will but tell me what I have done amiss,' she persisted.

'For goodness' sake, child, do you think I am petty enough to hold grudges about your nonsense?' he exploded.

'You'd best leave him be,' Clinton intervened, eyeing the other man coldly.

'He is clearly determined not to be pleased with anything you say.'

Kate glanced at Hawksley, afraid of his reaction. His lips parted, but then he pressed them closed again.

Clinton, fortunately, was not a quarrelsome man and, to try to restore the peace, he begged Kate to play something for him.

She agreed, though she was not in the mood for music. She glanced at Hawksley's morose expression as she took her place at the piano and unconsciously began playing one of his favourite tunes. She looked up frequently to gauge his reaction, but he turned his back to her.

Clinton and Mrs Buckingham praised her enthusiastically when she was done, but she willingly gave up her place to Orinda. Hawksley was still loitering by the window.

'I suppose you are the only person in this room who is likely to give me an unbiased opinion,' she said, glancing up at him with a shy smile, which froze at his look of deep displeasure.

'I would advise you to pay more attention to what you are doing if you wish to be praised.' Kate flinched. Had her performance been so terrible — or was it something else? She curtseyed and was about to withdraw without another word when he added, 'You can do much better than that — it pains me to see you waste your talents.'

'I am sorry I have displeased you.' She raised her chin and swished away too quickly to see a twinge of remorse cross his face.

6

A heavy shower the following morning stranded the whole party at Fairfield Hall and no one seemed in the best of humours. It took all of Kate's courage to approach Hawksley and ask him to help her with a difficult passage in the piece she intended to play at the concert.

'I am flattered you saw fit to spare me a little of your precious time.'

Kate caught fire at his words and retorted with, 'I'm sorry to be a nuisance. I shan't bother you again.'

'Don't be silly, child. Come here.'

She obeyed reluctantly, but she couldn't seem to grasp what he wanted of her. She was conscious that although the piano stood at the far end of the drawing room, every single exchange that passed between her and Hawksley must be audible to the others. Euphemia, in particular, was no doubt enjoying the spectacle.

She was almost at the end of her tether by the time Clinton suddenly exclaimed, 'The sun is out at last. We have time for a walk to the lake before dinner, do we not?' Everyone assented eagerly, apart from the pair at the piano. 'You are coming too, Miss Spenser?' Clinton urged.

Kate found her eyes drifting towards the window. The temptation was strong. The whole world was sparkling and washed clean by the rain and her head was muzzy from being confined indoors.

'We were in the middle of a lesson,' Hawksley intervened.

'Can you not let her off this once?' Clinton asked with his friendliest smile. 'You are more than welcome to join us.'

'I have no objection on my own account,' Hawksley replied, 'but I have my doubts whether the distance is not too great for Miss Spenser.'

'My ankle is much better,' Kate replied, irritated by his tone. What sort of invalid did he take her for?

'So you tell us,' he agreed, 'but I saw you limping yesterday after you returned from that walk to the village.'

'It was nothing, really.' She became flustered for she did not think anyone had noticed.

'It was bad enough to make you turn pale and spend the rest of the day on the sofa.'

'I'll go and fetch my hat,' Kate replied stubbornly, but the blood was pounding in her head. She had no idea that Hawksley had been watching her so closely.

As usual, Euphemia did not help. In the privacy of her room, she sympathised vociferously with Kate and did not allow her a moment to think.

'Really, Kate — Hawksley is just far too arrogant for a mere piano teacher. Perhaps I should I ask Papa to send him away forthwith?' she simpered.

'You needn't do that.' The thought made her panic. 'He is a very good teacher, after all.'

'You have such a sweet and forgiving nature. I cannot imagine why Hawksley hates you so much.'

'He does not hate me. He simply thinks I do not work hard enough.' But misery curled tight inside Kate. What if it was true? She mustn't cry, mustn't give Euphemia the satisfaction of seeing how unhappy she was. Her feelings were still in turmoil as she swept downstairs. Most of the party had gathered in the hall. No one seemed sure whether John Hawksley was coming with them or not, but melancholy music was emanating from the drawing room.

Kate did not know whether she ought to intrude. She owed Hawksley a good deal. He had invested his time, his talent, his limited stock of patience in her. And he had trusted her with his deepest secret. She could not forget happier days when they had worked well together, or the times he had held her in his arms when she was injured.

She opened the door softly. He did

not seem to hear her and continued playing. 'Won't you come with us?' she asked.

'You do not want me there.'

'That is not true, sir. We have had pleasant walks before this, have we not? Is there something preying on your mind? You have been much withdrawn these past days.'

'By which you mean I have been bad-tempered and moody,' he replied.

'Well, perhaps I do, but I know you are not always like that.' Kate spoke in her gentlest voice.

'I do not deserve your kindness.' His eyes took on a misty, yearning look she could not decipher. 'I wish . . . ' The words had uncommon energy, but he stifled whatever emotion it was that agitated him. In any case, they were interrupted by Frederick Clinton.

'Ready, Miss Spenser?' he asked cheerfully.

Kate glanced from one man to the other, torn. The frown had returned to Hawksley's face. 'I wonder . . . perhaps

I ought to stay,' she murmured. 'The concert is not far away and I have so few opportunities to practise.'

'Why on earth do you need to practise? Your music is perfect already. The whole world will be in ecstasies,' Clinton enthused.

'You flatter me,' Kate said, removing her hat. 'But there are other, less partial critics I must please.' She fixed her eyes on Hawksley.

'It will not be the same without you,' Clinton pleaded. 'And this fine weather cannot last long. Have you not been trapped long enough inside?'

But Kate managed to resist his temptations, though Euphemia's mock concern about her health almost made her change her mind. Hawksley barely acknowledged their presence, waiting for their departure with his back half-turned.

Clearly Hawksley felt as awkward as she. His commands were abrupt and he seemed restless. Kate found her concentration slipping, wondering what the others were doing. A few weeks ago, she would have been glad for any excuse to be alone with Hawksley, but his attitude made her tense and she half-resented her decision to stay behind.

'Have you heard a single word I have said?' Hawksley's voice cut through her reveries and made her jump.

'I'm sorry. I . . . '

'Do you remember our agreement? That if you proved difficult or inattentive, you would repay me for the time I have invested in you?' Kate began another apology, but Hawksley ranted on. 'Ever since Clinton arrived, your music has been neglected, your playing has become careless and you have seized every excuse to avoid lessons. Do you want to be a good pianist, or merely a dilettante?'

'Of course I wish to perform well,' Kate protested. 'And I do know there are sacrifices to be made.'

'Do you? My reputation is at stake too, you know, now that I have boasted to the world about how talented you are.'

Kate flushed. 'I did not know you had done so.'

'Would it have made you work harder if you had known? Or would you simply have rested on your laurels, trusting to your youth and beauty to make an impression, assuming that talent without hard work is enough?'

She could no longer contain herself and sprang to her feet. 'You really are as impossible as everyone says!' Kate hurled the words at him. 'I cannot talk to you when you are like this. And to think I defended you!'

She strode towards the door, but he reached it at the same time as she did and pushed it closed. Turning to face him, Kate found herself pinned against the door, his hands placed on the wooden panels on either side of her. His face was so close to hers that for an absurd moment, she thought he was about to kiss her.

'I have not asked you to defend me,'

he said. 'If you want to fritter away your talent, go ahead. But if you walk out of this door, do not expect me to teach you ever again.' He drew back two steps and his arms dropped to his sides, leaving her free to go.

'You are not the only music teacher in the world,' she said defiantly.

'No, but I am the best you are likely to get and the only one within travelling distance. Or perhaps you think it does not matter any more and that puppy will marry you? Pah! He cannot even decide which of the three of you he likes best. I have heard him confess it to Buckingham.'

His words were a shock to Kate. She was so used to every man being in love with Euphemia, that she had never seriously considered Frederick Clinton as a suitor.

'I thought you were not like other women, but you are nothing but a husband-hunting butterfly.'

Blind instinct took over. Kate lashed out with her hand, but he caught her wrist just short of her target and forced her arm down by her side.

'What business is it of yours whom I marry? You are not my father or my guardian or my brother!' Kate lifted her chin in a show of spirit and, if anything, his grip tightened. 'Or perhaps you think I should marry you?'

She saw something twitch in his face, a momentary spasm of pain, and she was glad she had managed to elicit this much of a reaction from him. And then a wave of shame overwhelmed her. Her words, revealing her innermost longings, would have been improper even if she had not known about his tragic past.

In a sudden wave of regret she flustered. 'Forgive me. I should not have said such a thing.'

There was something calm and deep and frightening in his eyes. Something so powerful she felt crushed under its weight. Abruptly he turned away, dropping her throbbing wrist. Looking down, she saw long, red finger marks on her skin.

Flicking back the skirts of his frock coat, Hawksley sat down at the piano and began to play the sonata he had written for his dead sweetheart.

Kate's hand closed round the door-knob, but she did not have the power to go. Instead she leaned against the door. She would have known he had not played that piece for a long time, even if he had not already told her so. But despite his mistakes — or perhaps because of them — the emotion he put into the piece was unmistakable.

He still loves her. He always will. No one will ever take her place. Kate found she was physically shaking, almost crying by the time the last note finally faded away.

A long silence descended on the room. She could hear her own breathing, shallow and ragged, as if she was sobbing. Out of the corner of her eye, she was aware that Hawksley was still sitting at the piano, his head bowed, his shoulders slumped forward, arms hanging loosely as if totally bereft of strength.

At length he rose from the piano and she hastily turned her head to hide the fact she had been watching him. She could feel his gaze on the nape of her neck and she knew that if she intended to go, this was her last chance.

It took every ounce of her strength to push open the door.

★ ★ ★

Kate fled, blinded by tears. She did not know where she was going. All she knew was that she had to get away. The haunting tune echoed round her head. How could she let it come to this? Hawksley did not want her or need her. She could never replace his dead sweetheart, nor rival Euphemia.

As she plunged out of the door into the garden, a figure loomed up in front of her. She gasped and shrank back, illogically convinced it must be Hawk-sley. A pair of hands caught her shoulders to steady her.

'Miss Spenser, what on earth is the matter?'

It was Frederick Clinton. Stunned by the suddenness of the encounter, Kate could not utter a single word, but merely tried to suppress her sobs.

'It's Hawksley, isn't it? What has he done to you now?' Clinton's vehemence startled Kate into looking up at him.

'N-nothing,' she stammered, but clearly he did not believe her.

'I know not why you allow him to bully you as he does,' he went on, his scowl deepening. 'The man is a brute. You have only to say the word and I shall call him out.'

Kate could not repress a cry of horror. A duel was the last thing she wanted, especially between these two men.

'No, you mustn't! Please promise me you will not do anything so rash.' Kate's mind strayed to her lost days of happiness. 'Think of the scandal.'

'Hawksley needs to know you are not defenceless and alone,' Clinton persisted, his eyes glimmering with a feverish light. He forced a smile despite the tight muscles in his cheeks and jaw. 'Will you not give me the right to protect you?'

Kate felt a jolt, knowing instinctively what was to come, but apparently incapable of preventing it. She was much too confused to know whether she wanted him to go on.

'Sir . . . ' she began ineffectually.

'My dear Miss Spenser, you must know how much I admire you,' Clinton went on impetuously. 'I know we have not known each other very long, but I wondered whether you might be . . . fond enough of me to accept my proposal for your hand in marriage?'

The reversal was too sudden; Kate's tears were not yet dry and her grief had not subsided. She had always liked Frederick Clinton, yet some instinct warned her not to rush into this decision. It was not so very long since she had allowed herself to hope that John Hawksley might come to care for her once he had discovered Euphemia's true character, but here was Clinton, gazing at her eagerly, tenderly, anxiously.

'I . . . I . . . like you very much, Mr Clinton,' Kate stammered, 'but you have taken me by surprise. I do not know what to say.'

'But you are not refusing me?' He instantly leapt at her words, clasping her hand tightly.

'N-no, I am not refusing, but . . . but I should like some time to consider . . . '

'Of course, of course — however long is necessary — only I beg you, do not say no in the end.'

Kate dropped her head, not knowing how to reply. The thought flashed across her mind. *What on earth would Euphemia say?*

7

Kate and Euphemia had retired to dress for the evening, but Kate realised she had been gazing blankly out of the window instead.

'Whatever is the matter with you?' Euphemia demanded. 'You have been in a daze all day.'

'It's nothing, truly. I am just tired, is all.'

But Euphemia was not to be fobbed off so easily. She eyed Kate shrewdly until her maid obscured her vision by lifting her upper petticoat over her head. That was something Kate always found disconcerting. Euphemia was so used to the maid's presence, she behaved as if she was not there, talking as intimately as if they were alone. For that reason alone Kate had never confided in her much.

However, Euphemia's intervention

had one positive effect. It reminded Kate she ought to make an effort to change too.

'You are keeping secrets from me,' Euphemia said, emerging from the folds of silk and shivering as the cooler air touched her skin. She crept up close behind Kate. 'Could it be that someone is in love?'

Kate jumped, even though she had been half expecting this. 'And with whom am I supposed to be in love?' she asked with false brightness in hopes of covering a guilty blush.

'Lah, I swear I would not know. Perhaps a certain gentleman whose name begins with C . . . ?' Euphemia's tone proved she was less unconcerned than she was pretending to be. The maid looked studiously busy, but Kate could see her ears prick.

'Mr Clinton and I are friends, nothing more,' she replied primly.

'By which you mean he has not yet proposed and you dare not admit it.'

Her self-satisfied tone made Kate's

hackles rise. Before she had time to consider what she was doing, she laughed airily and said, 'As a matter of fact, Mr Clinton has proposed, but I have not yet given him an answer.'

Euphemia's colour faded so suddenly, Kate was afraid she might faint. Whatever had induced her to say that?

Kate knew she had done the unforgivable in Euphemia's eyes by being the first to ensnare an eligible man — and one Euphemia had been toying with herself. The very thought of what she might do made Kate feel sick.

For the moment, Euphemia merely shrugged and said, 'I suppose I ought to congratulate you. I never expected you to make such a prudent match.'

'I have not yet accepted.' Kate felt it necessary to justify herself.

'Oh, but you must. Anything else would be sheer folly,' Euphemia purred. 'A girl in your position cannot cast aside a fortune of a few thousand a year.'

Kate tried to change the subject, but

even after they had joined the others, Euphemia kept making sly references to mercenary marriages. Why did Kate feel so guilty — and what did it matter what Euphemia believed or said? But no matter what she told herself, unease gnawed at Kate's heart.

It was not long after the ladies had left the dining room that John Hawksley became aware that Clinton was drinking more than usual. But instead of growing noisier, he drew deeper and deeper into himself.

'What the devil is the matter with you?' Rafe Buckingham asked, slapping him on the shoulder. 'Anyone would think you'd lost a thousand guineas at cards.'

There were a good many guests that night and neither man seemed to notice that Hawksley was listening.

'I have taken a gamble, that's a fact,' Clinton replied with a tight smile.

'What was it? Horses? Dice?' Rafe mocked. 'Or is there a woman involved, perchance?' Clinton's silence struck

Hawksley as suspicious. Clearly Rafe thought so too, for he uttered a low whistle. 'There is a woman, is there not?'

Clinton grinned uneasily. 'You had best congratulate me,' he said. 'For I have put my head in the noose — or as good as.'

'Made up your mind at last then, have you, you rogue? Which one is it to be — Effie or Rinda?'

'Neither — it's Miss Spenser. But you are not to tell a soul, since she has not yet given me an answer.'

'But she is hardly likely to say no, now, is she?'

Hawksley heard no more. *Too late, too late, too late!* The words hammered through his mind — and he knew he had only himself to blame.

*   *   *

Kate had never heard Hawksley play as passionately as he did that night. That alone told her that his calm exterior hid a whirlwind of emotion. Afterwards he was so besieged by admirers, she could not get near him. And what could she have said, after the way their last lesson had ended?

Frederick Clinton spent most of the evening by her side. He did his best to entertain her, but once or twice she caught him gazing at Euphemia, who was at her most arch and playful.

Kate knew her future hung in the balance. Clinton offered her all the security she could wish for. There was no reason why she should not be happy with him. He was so good-humoured, a far wiser choice for a husband than someone as moody as Mr Hawksley.

Dear God, what was she allowing herself to think now? Hawksley had never proposed to her. He was not in love with her. The impropriety made her squirm. And yet she could not shake the feeling that something dark overshadowed her.

No, she could not marry Clinton. It was as simple as that. Even if Hawksley never proposed, never cared for her except as his pupil, she could not marry Frederick Clinton. And since that was the case, it was not fair to keep him dangling.

'You look tired, Miss Spenser,' Clinton said.

'The noise is giving me a headache,' Kate confessed.

'Perhaps we can find somewhere a little quieter.'

He held the door open and Kate slipped out into the empty hall. By wordless consent, they strolled to the window and gazed at the moon through the branches of a vast oak that overshadowed the driveway.

'Such a beautiful night,' he said.

'Yes.' Kate hesitated, trying to find the words. 'Mr Clinton . . . '

'Won't you call me Frederick?' he whispered, taking her hand.

Kate's heart plummeted. He thought she was going to accept.

'I cannot, I must not . . . '

A door sprang open and cut off her

next words, and Clinton too had begun to speak. They both turned sharply towards the newcomer. Kate felt Hawksley's eyes alight on her face and slide down to her hand, still clasped loosely in Clinton's.

'I beg your pardon. I did not intend to intrude,' he said and withdrew.

A cry escaped Kate, but it was far too late to stop him, and anyway, there was nothing she could say to him.

'Miss Spenser, Catherine, you cannot mean what I think you mean.' Clinton's voice made her jump. She had almost forgotten he was there. 'You cannot mean to reject me.'

'I'm sorry. I am most flattered, of course, that you think well enough of me to make this offer, but . . . ' What reason did she have to give him? He was young, good-looking, rich, kind, amusing. *Why can I not love him? Life would be so much simpler as his wife.*

All she could do was gasp, 'I'm sorry, I'm sorry!' before tearing herself free and fleeing upstairs. Even there, her privacy would be short-lived. Sooner or later Euphemia would come to torment her.

Kate ripped off her gown and buried herself under the covers. No matter how much noise Euphemia made, no matter what happened, she would feign sleep. She could not bear anything more that night.

★　★　★

Kate's heart quickened as she entered the drawing room the next morning. She had spent the whole night fretting about the proposal. How on earth would she face Clinton now — or John Hawksley, for that matter?

She groaned when she remembered her conversation with Euphemia the previous evening. And what about the forthcoming concert — suppose Hawksley stuck to his word and refused to teach her?

She soon discovered that Euphemia was only too pleased to monopolise

Clinton's attention while throwing the occasional triumphant look at Kate. But the other dilemma was not so easily resolved. Kate tried to lure Hawksley to her by playing the piano. But even when she struggled over a difficult passage, he did not lift his head from the newspaper he was pretending to read.

At about noon, a black-edged letter arrived, announcing the death of her great-aunt.

'Never mind, my dear,' Mrs Buckingham murmured sympathetically. 'Perhaps my news will cheer you up. How would you like to come with us when we go to London for the Season?'

'That's very generous,' Kate stammered, 'but I am uncertain I can go.' The Buckinghams would absorb many of the expenses, like lodgings and transport, but she would need new clothes and a little spending money if she did not want to look too rusticated.

'Oh, but you must. Mr Hawksley was sure you would enjoy going to the

Opera and the concerts at the Pantheon.'

'Mr Hawksley?'

'Yes, it was his idea. I was so ashamed I did not think of it myself. You will never be wed if you stay here all your life.'

Kate scarcely heard her. She had thought that, after all the quarrelling, Hawksley would be only too pleased to get away from her, and yet he was still exerting himself on her behalf.

But he avoided her all day, denying her the chance to thank him.

★ ★ ★

She got up early the following morning, determined to confront Hawksley before the others were up. He was not in the drawing room and a cursory scout round the garden revealed no trace of him. She circled back to the piano, judging that was her best chance of luring him to her, and if he did not come, at least she would have used her time profitably.

She played for a long time to no

128

avail. In the end, she became so absorbed, she did not hear the door open. Her head was throbbing from lack of sleep and she was just about to give up when an impatient voice snapped, 'How on earth have you managed to get the rhythm so mangled? I do not believe you have gotten it right even once, today or yesterday.'

Kate flushed. So Hawksley had been listening after all. 'Perhaps if you had offered to help me then, I would not be in such a mess now.'

'Perhaps if you made time for lessons, the problem would never have arisen. Play it again.'

Kate threw him a half-defiant look. She had been in a conciliatory mood, but now his temper and her headache made her less tolerant than usual.

Nevertheless, she began to play, only to be stopped again at the third note.

'No, no, no! Let me show you.'

She rose to allow him to take her place. He repeated the phrase several times, before continuing the piece of music. She watched, fascinated by his long, elegant fingers moving up and down the keyboard. He looked up, caught her eye and broke off suddenly. 'Now you try it.'

She resumed her place, but felt painfully aware of how close he was behind her. She wiped her hands by pretending to spread out her skirts, brushed loose strands of hair out of her face, toyed with her ring and fidgeted until he snapped, 'Hurry up, child. I'm sure you are perfectly ready.'

With each moment she was growing more nervous. When he was in this mood, he was never easy to work with. But she could hardly send him away and arrange another time for their lesson. This might be her only opportunity.

Kate positioned her fingers on the keys. Tentatively she touched the first note and sprang back when the sound came out louder than she had anticipated. Hawksley sighed and, taking a deep breath, Kate tried again, but so timidly that half the notes were inaudible.

Hawksley tapped his foot against the floor and barely repressed a cutting comment. His impatience served only to make Kate more nervous. She steeled herself and made a slightly more connected effort, but lapsing into the incorrect rhythm again.

'I should have thought even you could remember what I told you for more than five minutes at a time,' Hawksley said. 'Again, right hand only.' He tapped out the rhythm on the top of the piano. Kate obeyed, then waited. 'Repeat it until I tell you to stop.'

After a while Hawksley grunted. Kate jumped when he laid his right hand on her shoulder for support and, leaning over her, positioned his left hand on the keys. 'Now play it again.'

She broke down halfway through the phrase. His proximity was simply too much for her. His hand tightened on her shoulder, rumpling her sleeve and she could feel his breath in her hair, but he compelled her to repeat the same phrase until she managed to play it to his accompaniment.

'Now the left hand,' he demanded. She practised the accompaniment until he was grudgingly satisfied and ordered her to repeat the phrase with both hands together. At length he growled, 'Better. Again.'

She was not concentrating and missed a note entirely. 'I have a terrible headache,' Kate pleaded, at the end of her tether by now.

'If you do not practise that phrase correctly now, you will lapse back into your old ways.' She persevered, hoping he would take pity on her. After four or five correct attempts, she glanced up at him. 'Again, child!'

'I am not a child!' Kate sprang to her feet, but he caught her by the shoulder and pushed her back onto the stool.

'Then do not behave like one.'

With difficulty, Kate choked down a surge of temper and tried a different tack. 'I am tired, sir. I have been practising for nearly two hours.'

'Then you can imagine how weary I am of listening to your blunders,' he retorted, his lips tightening as she winced under his iron grip. 'Believe me, I am as anxious as you to complete this lesson, but upon my oath, you shall not leave this room until you have played that phrase correctly ten times in a row, then the whole line that precedes it, then the whole page without a single mistake, even if we both have to go without breakfast, dinner and supper before you manage it.'

Kate glared at him, but she could see that he meant every word he said. She could imagine being kept at work all day, repeating the same phrase, until he got what he wanted.

'Proceed.'

But the more she tried, the less she seemed able to do it. Small mistakes she had never made before crept in. Her fingers became entangled. Her head grew more confused. Sometimes she managed the phrase correctly seven or eight times before making a mistake. Once she even managed nine times, breathlessly counting, but her nerve broke and the tenth time was so dreadful, she burst into tears.

Hitherto Hawksley had only uttered single words, like, 'Again' or, 'Better'. Now he uttered a disbelieving laugh. Kate's head sank into her hands, but he snatched the nearest one away from her face.

'Do not snivel, child. It's bad for the instrument. Continue, if you please. The sooner you perform it correctly, the sooner you can go.'

But Kate was beyond that now and her sobs increased. He watched her a moment before he placed his knee on the stool beside her and took her chin in one hand. 'Dry your eyes,' he said, striving to sound more patient. He brushed her tears away with the back of his hand and Kate shivered at his touch. 'I'm sorry.'

He let go of her chin, but remained half-kneeling beside her, one hand on each of her shoulders, as he had on her first morning at Fairfield Hall, when she had been so happy. She could feel his trembling energy and she realised that, for whatever reason, he too was close to collapse.

She tried again and though her touch was wavering, she was almost correct. Encouraged, she persisted, trying to ignore his grip on her shoulders. She lost count of how many times she repeated the phrase and eventually glanced up at him.

'Do not stop now,' he said. 'I told you I want to hear the whole line, and now you appear to have mastered the difficulty, you had better take it from the beginning of that bar.'

He leaned closer to her to point to the place, then just as abruptly pulled away and began pacing about the room. She played the first part of the line, but came to a sudden halt before the phrase she had practised so much.

'As it was when you practised it separately. Listen and think about what you are doing.' He sang the phrase and beat the rhythm against the top of the piano. As Kate got to the difficult phrase, he tapped out the rhythm with her. 'Better. Again.'

She could feel the tension in his voice. Her head was throbbing. Each time she played the line, it grew hazier in her mind until she hardly knew what she was doing.

'Now from the top of the page.'

'Please sir, I am so tired . . .'

'We are nearly done.'

She was too exhausted to argue. Almost blindly, she began to play. She managed the difficult section, then her fingers tripped over an easy phrase and a terrible discord cut through her heavy head. Appalled by the blunder, she fumbled to correct it, but only made matters worse.

'What the devil are you doing?'

His fist crashed against the top of the piano with such force that a heavy brass candlestick that had been left on it rocked and tumbled forward onto Kate.

Notes clashed and Kate cried out in pain, snatching her hands to her bosom a fraction of a second too late and the candlestick struck her hand.

She did not see John Hawksley freeze. His lips trembled. His fist unclenched and dropped by his side. His breast heaved as though he was contending with some terrible demon within.

Kate's eyes flashed upward at his broken cry. Her vision blurred with tears. She started back as he dropped to his knees before her and seized her hands. With a metallic thud, the candlestick rolled from her lap, onto the carpet and under the piano.

'Kate!' he groaned. 'My darling, my love, forgive me! I never meant to hurt you. Oh, God, what have I done?'

Hawksley lifted her hands to his lips, kissing each finger in turn, gently manipulating each joint, begging her to tell him if anything hurt, if anything was broken. Too shocked even to cry, Kate stared at his bowed head through a film of unshed tears.

He loves me! She kept repeating the sentence, but still it did not seem real. She had not been wasting her love on someone who merely regarded her as his pupil. He had been so hard on her, not because he despised her, but because he was trying to keep his emotions hidden. If he had been jealous of Frederick Clinton, it was for her sake, not Euphemia's.

'Please get up.' Her right hand tingled beneath the tender, urgent pressure of his lips. His shoulders shook and she heard his breath grow ragged. 'I forgive you. It was merely an accident. Please get up.'

She rose, tugging at his hands that still clasped hers. Hawksley staggered blindly to his feet and for a moment she glimpsed the raw emotion in his face, the love she had sometimes seen in his eyes without realising what it was, or that it was directed at her. Something in her expression caused him to pull away. She tried to keep hold of his hands, but he was too strong.

'Wait!' she called after him, though she did not know what she could say to him that was proper, but yet would still let him know that his feelings were not unreciprocated.

He stopped by the door, his back towards her. 'Please, let me go,' he said in a husky voice. 'If you have any mercy, let me go,' he repeated.

He seemed so distressed, she could not deny his request, though she would far rather have put her arms around his neck and consoled him that way. Only propriety kept her rooted to the spot. 'Very well.'

He opened the door, but could not resist a single glance back at her. Kate had turned aside to put away the music, but sensing his eyes upon her, she looked up. She was only just in time to see him whisk away, closing the door firmly behind him.

A gleam caught her eye. Kate stooped to pick up the candlestick and put it back in its place. She allowed her fingers to slide down it from its lip, over the decorative rings to the bell-shaped base. The pain in her hand had settled into a dull ache and she was scarcely aware of it any more. She suspected a bruise would appear on the back of her hand before the day was out, but not even the skin was broken. Her fingers might be stiff at first, but she trusted that would pass before the concert.

The concert. She would make Hawksley proud of her at the concert. She was sure love and happiness would make her play better than she had ever done, and afterwards he would draw her aside for a quiet word and his praise would mean more than anything else in the world . . . She had almost forgotten about her headache, but now it hit her with a violent dagger blow to the forehead. She didn't care. *He loves me.*

8

Those words continued to haunt her long after John Hawksley had left. She missed having the privacy of her own room, but did not dare go out into the garden for fear of encountering Hawksley when he had asked her to stay away. Instead she took refuge in the library, knowing she was less likely to be interrupted there than in the drawing room.

She should have guessed. She could not believe she had been so stupid. She had been misled by Euphemia's assertions. Could her so-called friend have been mistaken, or was there a more sinister explanation? Kate struggled to reassess everything that had happened to her since her arrival at Fairfield Hall.

She felt a sudden pang of longing for her mother and the security of Fairfield Cottage. And yet she suspected that even if her mother had been at home, she would not have told her what had passed between her and John Hawksley that morning.

Just a few more days before she could go home. A few more days in which to try to make things right with Hawksley. She had handled the situation badly, taken too much by surprise. He probably felt humiliated by his loss of self-control. She wished now she had given way to impulse and made him stay and talk to her. She had said and done nothing to convince him that his feelings were reciprocated. Perhaps she should have gone after him. Was it too late? She was still undecided at breakfast, but resisted an urge to seek solitude. She had to see him again so she could judge what he was thinking. Even being in the same room as him would be bliss, now she knew that he loved her.

But John Hawksley did not come to breakfast or send any excuse for his absence. Kate felt obliged to stay with the others, taking little part in their amusements, but wishing to be present when Hawksley returned.

She raised her head frequently from her sewing, hoping to catch a glimpse of him through the window, crossing the lawn towards the house. Her ears strained for the thud of the front door or the click of footsteps in the hall. At times it was all she could do to keep her seat.

He did not return until they had retired to dress for dinner. Despite Euphemia's incessant chatter, Kate's quick ear caught the sound of Hawksley's voice in the hall, too far away to discern any words. She paused near the door, listening to his steps come up the stairs. But he was neither bounding energetically nor dragging his feet, giving her no indication of his state of mind.

Conversing with Euphemia was an ordeal. She insisted that she was delighted that Kate might come with them to London. But at the same time, she bemoaned how very expensive everything had grown and how even Papa's generous allowance was scarcely enough to keep her in clothes.

London. Kate had been comparatively indifferent to Mrs Buckingham's invitation before, but now she was desperate to go. London was where Hawksley would be during the long months of the fashionable season. But Euphemia was right. She could not possibly afford to go.

* * *

Kate paused on the threshold. Her eye fell instantly upon John Hawksley, though he was at the far end of the drawing room, talking to Mr Buckingham. Candlelight added a warm glow to his cheek and she was overwhelmed by a sudden awareness of how handsome he was. Could a man like that really be in love with her?

A tug on her arm roused her. Euphemia had insisted that they should enter the room together, arm-in-arm as in the olden days. Now Kate realised Frederick Clinton had just said something to them, but she had no idea what it was. But Euphemia was laughing prettily, so Kate commandeered a smile.

As the evening progressed, Kate formed the impression that John Hawksley was deliberately staying as far away from her as possible. Only now and then she caught him gazing at her from across the room, often just after she had laughed at one of Clinton's sallies.

It took her by surprise that Frederick Clinton was so unchanged. After some initial awkwardness, he behaved as though nothing had happened. It was only after dinner that she noticed that Mrs Buckingham seemed distracted, but there was no opportunity to ask if anything was wrong.

'Oh, Mr Hawksley.' Mrs Buckingham's face partially cleared at the sight of him. She gave him her most beseeching smile. 'I wanted to ask you — is it true you are leaving us?'

Kate's heart skipped a beat. Her eyes flew to his face. She suspected he was aware of her gaze because, although he avoided looking directly at her, he flushed. 'Only for a few days,' he replied. 'Urgent business in Bath.'

It was quite clear to Kate from his tone that he did not want to discuss the matter any further, but Mrs Buckingham would not let it drop. 'Oh, but you will be back in time for the concert?' she gushed. 'I am certain you would hate to miss that.'

'I'm afraid I cannot be certain of anything at this stage,' he said.

He changed the subject, but Kate kept darting surreptitious looks at him. She snatched the opportunity to speak to him when Mrs Buckingham was called away. 'I hope you are not running from me,' she said in a whisper.

'Not all the world revolves around you, Miss Spenser.'

It was her turn to flush. She

remembered that a letter had arrived for him that afternoon. 'That was not my intended meaning. Of course you must have more pressing engagements. But . . . you will be at the concert?'

'You do not need me there.'

'Yes, I do. I . . . I shall fall apart, I know I will.'

'Then it is time I cut the ties. It was never part of the plan to make you dependent upon me.'

'But . . . ' She was silenced, held prisoner by his intense gaze. Her house of cards toppled. What had she expected? He had not proposed to her and she had been premature in supposing that he would. She had never begged a man before and she felt humiliated because she had played upon his feelings for her and he had rejected her. Or perhaps she was mistaken. Perhaps he did not love her after all.

'I did not realise that by being so strict I was undermining your confidence as a musician,' he said softly.

'Clearly it was a mistake and I am very sorry for it.'

'No, you were right. My playing was lazy, undisciplined and self-indulgent. It is only that I might lapse into my old ways in your absence.'

'If you do and I catch you at it, there will be hell to pay,' he said with one of his rare smiles. Her heart jolted so suddenly, it made her feel faint. 'I have every confidence in you as a performer.'

'Thank you,' she murmured, but even this praise was not enough to drive away the sense of desolation that was growing stronger by the minute.

Later Kate realised they had been lucky to snatch enough time to say even this much. Mrs Buckingham begged Hawksley to play something for them, since he was to leave early the following morning. He insisted on playing duets with Euphemia and Orinda, before asking Kate to play a third. She could not help but be conscious of how close his foot was to hers, or the way their elbows touched occasionally. As she rose, his fingertips brushed against the bruise on her hand.

She lay awake for a long time that night. As a result she overslept and by the time she rose, John Hawksley had already gone.

★   ★   ★

'Do you not think you have practised long enough, Kate?'

'Just half an hour more, Mamma.'

Mrs Spenser sighed. 'In half an hour it will be dark. I really think you ought to come for a short walk. You are beginning to make mistakes because you are too tired.'

Kate considered arguing, but she had not the energy. Besides, she suspected her mother was right.

It was the day before the concert. Earlier, she had called at the hall with her mother and discovered that John Hawksley had neither written nor returned. The house was in a bustle of last-minute preparations. Euphemia was in her element, gliding about, countermanding her mother's orders, while Mrs Buckingham gazed at her, marvelling that she could have produced such a clever, beautiful and fashionable daughter.

Kate shivered. The evenings were growing chill. All sorts of worries that had receded while she was staying at Fairfield Hall now rushed back in full force. Could she make her old pelisse last another winter? And her winter boots needed to be re-soled.

'What is it, Kate?' her mother asked. 'You have done nothing but sit at that piano since I got home and Mrs Buckingham tells me you have been in low spirits for several days.'

'I simply wish to make a good impression at the concert, Mamma.'

They walked on in silence. The knowledge that John Hawksley would not be at the concert lay in the pit of Kate's stomach like a lump of ice. Indeed, there was every chance that he would never come back to Hereford-shire.

'Mrs Buckingham did wonder whether perhaps you had fallen in love,' her mother suggested gently. 'She tells me that you and Mr Clinton spent a good deal of time together.'

There had been dreams and half-conscious thoughts during the past nights, of hands touching, arms pulling her irresistibly against a man's chest, lips pressing against hers and gradually travelling downward. But the man in the dreams was not Frederick Clinton.

Perhaps her mother ought to know the truth, or part of it. 'Mr Clinton proposed to me but I refused him,' she said quietly.

'Kate!' Mrs Spenser was rendered momentarily speechless. 'Do you regret your decision?'

'No, Mamma. I like him very much, but I am not in love with him.'

'So you are certain there is nothing I can help you with?' her mother persisted. 'I hate seeing my only child unhappy.'

'I am not unhappy,' she lied, but could scarce credit it when her mother seemed to believe her.

'Did Mrs Buckingham tell you she has invited us to go with them to London?' Mrs Spenser tried another tack.

'Yes, but I know we cannot afford it, so . . .'

'But that's just it, Kate! My aunt left me a small sum of money — nothing spectacular, but enough for a month or two in London. Would you like that?'

It took Kate a moment to absorb the news. She had taken it for granted that she would be trapped in Herefordshire for the rest of her life. *In London I may see him again — he promised to call on Mrs Buckingham. Perhaps I will be given a second chance.* 'Yes, Mamma, I believe I would.'

★ ★ ★

By the time Kate and her mother reached Fairfield Hall for the concert, many of the guests had already arrived, though the more illustrious ones had deliberately delayed, simply to prove to the world that they were too important to be governed by clocks.

Euphemia spent much of her time simpering behind her fan and throwing luminous gazes at anyone of any importance. Frederick Clinton was particularly attentive. Once, when Orinda tried to lure him away to join her merry band of madcap girls, he looked tempted, but a single glance from Euphemia kept him captive. Kate ended up with Orinda's circle, because she knew few people present. She even managed briefly to forget that she was expected to perform, until a hush descended on the drawing room and Euphemia took her place at the piano.

Thereafter it would have taken a performer of the calibre of John Hawksley to distract Kate from the rumblings of unease in her stomach.

Orinda and her friends continued to gossip throughout the concert, but Kate could not concentrate on the music or the conversation.

At last her own turn came. She tried not to look at the massed heads of the audience or pick out any faces, because she knew she would lose her nerve completely. Her hands felt hot and sticky and she spread out her white skirts to give herself an extra moment to prepare. She had deliberately not worn any rings for fear they might slip and hamper her, and her hands looked very bare as she placed them on the keyboard. She noticed the bruise on the back of her right hand, now just a faded smudge, and she shuddered as she remembered the feel of Hawksley's kisses. Then she braced herself. Instead of thinking of things that could never be, she must try to keep all of Hawksley's injunctions in mind.

That night Kate played with unchar-acteristic precision. She could hear the notes hammered out, like the strokes of a bell. She did not dare let go of her emotions, afraid they might swamp her. What on earth would people think if she broke down and cried in the middle of her performance?

Instead she produced something immaculate, but without a soul. Her only consolation was that John Hawksley was not there to witness her performance. That thought alone drove her relentlessly towards the end.

Only after she had curtseyed to the polite applause was her eye attracted irresistibly to a tall figure at the far end of the room. She felt her soul shrivel under the steady gaze of those unmistakable grey eyes.

9

Every instinct told her to flee. But it was impossible to reach the main door without passing Hawksley and every other exit from the room was blocked by the audience.

As she passed down the aisle towards her seat, she could not help overhearing an elderly lady remark acidly to her friend, 'Well, my dear, I cannot say I was impressed.' She smirked. 'I was told this Spenser girl was truly exceptional, but I'd venture to say any young lady in the room could do as well.' Clearly she had no idea that the piece Kate had played was technically beyond the capabilities of most amateurs.

'I am as disappointed as you,' her friend concurred. 'Is it any wonder girls become swollen-headed when they are puffed up beyond their merits?'

Kate turned aside, feeling sick. She

did not want to stay until the end of the concert and was already formulating excuses about the stifling atmosphere making her ill, when a hand gently took her by the crook of her elbow. She gasped as she looked up at Hawksley's handsome features.

'Allow me,' he said.

They were near the back of the room and all attention was on the next performer. Nobody noticed Hawksley manoeuvre Kate out into the hall. She shivered. The air was deliciously cool, but she was totally alone with the one person she had hoped to avoid. She attempted to push past him back into the drawing room, but he barred her way.

'Say it quickly and have done,' she said, turning her face aside. 'I know exactly what you think of tonight's performance.'

'I doubt you do.'

'Shall I say it for you? I am a failure. I lost my nerve and probably always will. I am not fit to play in public. You have been very generous in the pains you have taken with me and I shall pay back every penny I owe you, if you will allow me a little time.'

'Shh.' He placed his forefinger on her lips and his touch made a shiver ripple through her body. 'There will be no talk of failure or debts in my hearing, is that understood?'

She threw him a half-resentful look. She chafed under the load of disappointment in herself, feeling that she had let down both her mother and her mentor.

'I'm afraid this is all my fault,' he said quietly. 'You were not ready yet,' he continued. 'I abandoned you too soon. But I wish you to know how extremely proud I am of you.'

'Proud, sir?' She stared at him through the half-dark. Was he mocking her? 'But you heard me play, you heard what everyone thought, you . . . '

'Yes, child, proud,' he reiterated. 'True, you let your nerves get the better of you. But do you remember how inaccurately you played when we first met, with at least one note missing in every chord?'

She squirmed, but he took her by both shoulders, forcing her to face him. She could not bring herself to look him in the eye and gazed at his waistcoat buttons instead.

'The hardest battle has been won. Technically I cannot fault tonight's performance. This concert was a triumph of a kind. Expression is natural to you but precision is not. I know you think you have sacrificed one for the sake of the other. If I thought this situation was irreversible, I would be wretched at having impaired your gift.'

Kate listened in silence, blinking back tears. John Hawksley must have felt her trembling, because he led her to the staircase and compelled her to sit down on the second step before seating himself beside her. Gently he turned her face towards him.

'With just a little more practice, this precision will become second nature and the expressiveness will return. And, believe me, that is what sets you apart from all those pampered moppets in there. Any donkey can learn the technique, if it is drilled mercilessly enough. But the gift you have cannot be taught and it will shine through, if you let it.' His deep grey eyes held hers captive. His touch on her cheek was gossamer-light. 'Within a week I believe you could make those vicious old tabbies eat their words.'

Kate blushed and looked down. She felt Hawksley's fingers run across her cheek. 'I do not know what to say.'

'Then say nothing.'

She felt his breath on her lips, coming closer and closer, and she raised her eyes to his face. Without warning he sprang to his feet.

'I must go,' he said, extending his hand to help her up. 'I am expected to play as a grand climax. But we must arrange some more lessons for you when you are in London.'

Kate felt as if she had been woken

too suddenly from a dream. 'You are not staying in Herefordshire?' she asked, dismayed.

'I cannot. I have other engagements . . . ' But he would not meet her eye.

Kate dropped her head, fighting to conceal her dejection. She did not trust her voice not to betray her feelings.

'Kate?' His voice was full of emotion.

'Yes?' She responded instinctively to that voice of all voices, and only belatedly realised that John Hawksley had called her by her first name. She turned towards him and before she had time to register how close he was, his arms had twined around her, drawing her towards him.

She raised her hands to ward him off, and yet somehow they remained flat against his chest as he lowered his head to hers. She knew she ought to turn away, and yet she did not. The kiss was tentative at first, but gradually increased in passion and intensity. Her head swam. She felt his hand glide up her back to settle on the nape of her neck, pressing her face to his shoulder. She nestled against him, her eyes closed. She could feel his chest rise and fall, the insistent throb of his heart. He breathed in slowly and she realised he was trying to inhale her scent, her very essence.

And then he tore himself away. He threw her a backward glance from the door, and for a moment she thought he would come back. She even began to extend her arms towards him, but she was mistaken. Perhaps a single word would have been enough to keep him there, but she did not find it in time, and then he was gone.

★   ★   ★

It was not until the next day that Kate realised the full significance of that kiss. It lingered on her lips long after it was over. When she woke, her first sensation was of being held warmly, tightly in his arms, his mouth striving and insistent upon her own.

She knew that if it happened again she ought to resist and keep him at arm's length until he declared his intentions. But she also knew how hard it would be to force the issue in case she drove him away. Shameful though it was, the blood pounding in her veins told her she would rather be John Hawksley's mistress than live without him.

She had loitered in the hall for several minutes after that kiss, confident that nobody would notice her absence. But the possibility that she might miss Hawksley's performance had driven her back into the drawing room.

She couldn't help noticing as he played that Hawksley looked pale and haggard after his recent journey. She allowed her eyes to travel over his forehead, down the curve of his cheek and jaw to his mouth, which was lightly compressed in a neutral expression. Her gaze lingered, remembering those lips against her own, and the mere thought made her tingle. She jumped as if she had been caught in a misdeed when his lashes swept upward and his grey eyes fixed on hers.

But Hawksley had not quite done with her. After a performance that had sent the audience into ecstasies, instead of playing a conventional encore, he had asked Kate to perform with him one of the duets they had practised during their stay at Fairfield Hall. Kate tried to resist, but somehow she found herself placing her hand in his and allowing herself to be led to the piano.

'Play as if you were playing only for me,' he murmured softly in her ear. 'Forget the others.'

She took a deep breath and plunged into the music, aware this might be her last opportunity to convey to Hawksley how much she loved him. It was as well her fingers knew the piece off by heart, because her eyes filled with tears as she poured her whole soul into the music. Throughout she was quiveringly aware of his proximity, his elbow brushing against hers, his fingers almost touching hers as their hands crossed over.

As the last notes faded away, Kate realised a deadly silence hung over the room. Such a thing had never happened to her before. Could they all have slipped away silently while they were playing? Half frightened, she raised her eyes, first to Hawksley, then the audience. They seemed frozen, stunned. Then a murmur rippled across the room and the applause began. Kate glanced at Hawksley again. She could see from his expression that he was deeply moved.

There had been no further opportunity to talk to Hawksley that evening. He had been so lionised, she could not get within a few yards of him. But her dismay at Hawksley's imminent departure had been tempered by the hope of seeing him again in London.

It was from Frederick Clinton that she had discovered Hawksley had only returned that afternoon, with barely enough time to change, eat and rest before the concert. 'Miss Buckingham was almost inconsolable, terrified of what the county families would say when they discovered Hawksley wouldn't be playing after all,' he said. 'I came upon her in tears in the summerhouse yesterday.' Kate could not help wondering if Euphemia had been aware of his presence before she started crying. She was one of those rare, enviable women who retained and even enhanced her beauty when she was in tears, instead of becoming blotched and swollen. 'She was close to throwing her arms about Hawksley's neck when she saw him clambering out of the carriage, all dusty and tired.'

'Surely not? I cannot imagine Miss Buckingham doing something so undignified,' Kate replied. 'Miss Orinda perhaps, but not — '

'Upon my honour,' Clinton insisted. 'Can you imagine how horrified poor Hawksley would have been at such a public display?'

She forced herself to laugh, trying not to wonder how John Hawksley would have reacted if she, Kate Spenser, had thrown her arms around his neck. She hastily changed the subject, but discovered Clinton was uncertain of the duration of Hawksley's present stay in Herefordshire.

'There has been some talk of his making a tour of the principal cities of Europe,' he added. It was a salutary reminder that Hawksley had another life, far away from here. He had been here such a short span, yet Kate had begun to take his presence for granted.

* * *

With a start, she realised she had lounged in bed much longer than usual. She rose in a hurry, afraid that Hawksley's impatience might cause him to call earlier than was his wont. But breakfast came and went without interruption. Kate turned down her mother's suggestion that they should go for a walk, for fear Hawksley would call while they were out. Instead she launched herself into her practice, to try to cheat away the minutes that dragged like hours. But he did not come.

Her unease had grown to an intolerable pitch by the time the knock came at the door. She jumped to her feet and stared in blank disappointment at the sight of Mrs Buckingham. She had forgotten that she had promised to call. Kate listened with only half an ear as Mrs Buckingham and her mother discussed the success of the previous evening and the forthcoming Season in London. All her senses were straining to catch the slightest hint of John Hawksley's approach. Surely, surely he would come soon.

'I am certain we are both very grateful to you for your generous invitation,' Mrs Spenser said. 'And we owe a great deal to Mr Hawksley.'

'That reminds me,' Mrs Buckingham said, producing a rolled up manuscript. 'Before he set out, Mr Hawksley asked me to give you this.'

Kate felt a cold shiver down her back. 'Set out?' she echoed faintly. A single glance revealed the manuscript was a musical score in Hawksley's handwriting, a copy of one of his own compositions.

'At dawn this morning,' Mrs Buckingham confirmed. 'I am not sure he even went to bed last night.' The chill oozed deeper and deeper into Kate's bones. Could he really have gone without saying goodbye? Mrs Buckingham looked at her with mild bemusement. 'Did you not know he was to tour Europe?' she asked. 'I did ask him how long he would be away, but he said he was not certain because one concert leads to another. If he finds a suitable appointment, he might never come back at all.'

Kate covered her mouth. She understood now. The kiss had not been a beginning, but an end. Not a declaration of love, but a farewell.

It was a relief when Mrs Buckingham finally departed and Kate could retreat to her room and bury her head beneath her pillow to muffle her sobs. It took a long time before she recovered sufficiently to examine the precious score. Suddenly she froze, then sat up straighter, brushing the tears out of her eyes. A letter had been slipped in between the other pages. Her heartbeat quickened in anticipation. It was not quite seemly for him to have written to her like this, but she hardly cared about such considerations. But at the first sentence she uttered an involuntary gasp. She sank back on the bed, the page quivering so much in her hand, she could hardly make out the words. Their meaning penetrated slowly; like blood oozing from a wound.

My dear Miss Spenser,

I wish to apologise for my unpardonable behaviour last night. I took advantage of the trust you and your mother have placed in me, and of that I am deeply ashamed. I am going abroad to fulfil some engagements I have there, because I know that if I remain within reach of you, I am liable to distress you by losing my self-control again.

My only excuse is that I have allowed myself to fall in love with you. I know I have no right to burden you with such confessions since I am in no position to offer to marry you. I have no wealth, no home and am little better than the plaything of my patrons, who may discard me whenever they choose. Miss Buckingham has told me how important it is for you to marry well and I hope that by teaching you I have been of some use to you.

This trifling composition was written with you in mind. I wish you every success and happiness for the future and I trust that by the time I return, you will be married to some agreeable, wealthy gentleman who will give you everything that I cannot.

Your sincere well-wisher,
J Hawksley

It was only then that Kate's eye alighted on the first page of the piece of music and she realised it was the sonata he had been writing since coming to Fairfield Hall.

10

There was an unreal feel to the weeks that followed. Kate found herself drifting around familiar haunts and resuming old routines, but Hawksley's absence had left a void inside her. She re-read his letter and practised his sonata until she knew both by heart. At nights she lay awake, re-playing that last scene, trying to find a way in which she could have prevented him from leaving, praying that he would not be able to stay away, plotting how she might see him again and what she would say to him if she did.

He did not return. Day followed day, and she pushed John Hawksley further back in her mind because she could see that tormenting herself would do no good. Yet, fool that she was, she felt compelled to scan newspapers for any snippet about his whereabouts, but was rarely rewarded for her pains. Those paragraphs she did find told her little, except that he had entertained such-and-such members of Parisian society or the Austrian aristocracy. They did not tell her whether he was well or happy.

Thoughts of him were revived in the bustle of Christmas and the subsequent move to town. Mrs Buckingham filled her townhouse with guests and was soon swamped with invitations in which Kate and her mother were included. Kate found there was little time to practise her music. Occasionally Mrs Buckingham mentioned Hawksley's name, wondering out loud where he might be, but nobody had any recent news of him and Kate assumed he must still be abroad.

Frederick Clinton had taken a house nearby for his widowed mother and was an assiduous visitor at the Buckinghams' townhouse. Mrs Clinton turned out to be a pallid cobweb of a woman, content to drift on every breeze and leaving the impression that a tempest would destroy her utterly, but Euphemia insisted on cultivating her acquaintance. In any case, Mrs Buckingham's kind heart would not have allowed her to neglect such a fragile neighbour.

Kate could not help noticing that, as the weeks passed, Euphemia's interest in Clinton seemed to wane. Perhaps it was inevitable when there were so many other admirers for her to choose from, some of them wealthier and more aloof than Clinton and therefore more of a challenge. Indeed the only thing that could revive her interest was if Clinton had the temerity to flirt with somebody else in her presence.

Euphemia had told Kate — 'strictly in confidence' — that she had had three offers of marriage in as many weeks since their arrival in London, but had neither accepted nor rejected any just yet, 'because it would be unwise to rush such an important decision, don't you agree?'

Privately Kate thought it unfair of Euphemia to keep her suitors dangling if she had no intention of accepting them. She also knew it would serve no purpose to say so and that Euphemia's true intention in confiding in her was to make Kate feel her inferiority in both wealth and beauty. However, considering that one of Euphemia's admirers was a sweet but terribly vague baronet and another a self-made man with a reputation for ruthlessness in both business and personal matters, Kate did not envy her much.

Euphemia's chief amusement was to provoke her suitors into displays of jealousy as she favoured one and then another. Occasionally Kate thought she had overplayed her hand, but whenever one of them seemed likely to stalk off in a huff, Euphemia would reel him back in with a sweet smile and some whispered mockery of his rivals.

The climax, Kate suspected, was likely to occur at a private ball to which they had all been invited. Euphemia made sure she was flanked by Kate and Orinda as she entered the ballroom, aware that her beauty would make her the most conspicuous figure in the group.

'So,' Orinda began with a teasing smile at her sister, 'which of your numerous suitors will you favour tonight?'

Euphemia fanned herself. 'I have not yet decided. It depends entirely upon how they comport themselves. It would be nice to be Lady Harrington, I suppose, though I believe he has not a penny to bless himself, and Mr Watson does have a vast fortune, but really, his is such a common name that I am not sure I could reconcile myself to adopting it.' Throughout her speech, Euphemia's fan continued to waft as she scanned the room, distributing smiles and nods and arch looks. 'Of course, I could accept Mr Clinton instead,' Euphemia went on, too casually. She flickered a malicious glance at her sister. 'Or would that break your heart utterly?'

Orinda coloured, but raised her chin defiantly. 'Why would it?'

'Oh, come, 'Rinda, it is quite obvious you are desperately in love with him. Such a shame he sees you as no more than an amusing little sister.'

Kate had expected Orinda to laugh off this accusation but, to Kate's horror, she saw Orinda's eyes fill with tears. Deliberately or by chance, Euphemia had struck a raw nerve. Kate wracked her mind for something to say, but it was too late. A familiar voice made them all start.

'Good evening, ladies,' Frederick Clinton said, showing no obvious signs that he had overheard their conversation. 'Might I have the honour of being your partner for the country-dances, Miss Orinda?'

The gracious smile wavered on Euphemia's lips. She had expected to be the first to be asked, but she recovered her self-possession with remarkable speed and seemed amused by her sister's stammered acceptance.

There was no chance for Kate to talk to either Buckingham sister after that because they were besieged by Euphemia's admirers. In the midst of the confusion, Kate was suddenly overwhelmed by the unsettling sensation of being watched. She turned her head and, with a shock, her gaze met with that of John Hawksley. He was at the opposite end of the room, but she expected him to bow or at least acknowledge her with a nod. Instead he turned away abruptly, as if pretending belatedly that he had not seen her.

Kate felt a cold wave sweep over her. She had thought the keenest edge of her feelings for Hawksley had worn off with the passage of time, but one glance at his face brought longing, bewilderment and anger surging back in equal measures. That last kiss still tingled on her lips, but clearly John Hawksley did not intend to acknowledge her, even as a former pupil.

Stung, Kate retreated within herself, relieved that Euphemia was far too busy to have observed that little exchange. But she felt painfully exposed while playing her minuet, sensing that Hawksley must be watching her, yet not daring to look, for fear she would make a mistake, or discover that he was either preoccupied or had left the room entirely.

But no one watched during the country-dances. She could lose herself amid the chaos of the longways set, dance as if her life depended on it, smile at her partner and her opposite as each dance dictated. The thought had crossed her mind that, while progressing along the set, she might encounter Hawksley, but evidently he was not a dancer and the hope that she might come within touching distance of him faded away.

Kate danced one dance after another, afraid of being left alone with her thoughts, afraid of being forced to accept that the man she was desperately in love with had cut her dead. And yet, sometimes, fleetingly, she thought she caught a glimpse of that unmistakable, soberly-clad figure, always situated so he could watch her. But she didn't have time to make certain that she was not deluding herself.

By suppertime her ankle, which had given her no trouble since summer, had started to throb. As her partner led her back towards her mother and Mrs Buckingham, they were joined by Orinda and Clinton. It was clear that any earlier awkwardness between them had been dissipated. Indeed Orinda's eyes glittered with suppressed excitement as she exclaimed, 'Oh, Kate, I am so glad you're here. I would not want you to miss my news.'

Kate conjured up a smile, though her steps faltered as she caught sight of the dark-clad figure conversing with Mrs Buckingham, but Kate knew she had no choice; she had to join the rest of her party.

'No, Mr Hawksley, I will not hear a word against it,' Mrs Buckingham was saying as they approached. 'You must call on us, must he not?'

Kate assumed it was pure coincidence that Mrs Buckingham turned to her in appeal, but she flushed nonetheless. 'Of course he is welcome,' she replied quietly, 'though there must be many calls upon his time.'

Kate was not sure anybody heard her. Her voice was drowned out by Orinda and Euphemia, who had joined them with her partner, the wealthy if lowly-born Mr Watson. But Mr Hawksley would make no promises and studiously avoided Kate's gaze.

'Oh, but you will come to the wedding, will you not?' Orinda cooed.

If she had wanted to create a sensation, she certainly succeeded. Hawksley looked up sharply, his narrowed eyes finding Kate instantly. Although Orinda had modestly dropped her gaze, Kate saw she was covertly peeping at her sister.

'I have asked Mr Buckingham for permission to marry his younger daughter and he has granted it.' Frederick

Clinton stepped into the breach.

'You have my heartiest congratulations,' Euphemia said with a meaningful look at Clinton. 'I only hope my sister's impulsiveness will be no bar to your future happiness.'

'Oh, I am so glad you're pleased.' Orinda tilted her chin defiantly. 'I was afraid it might be embarrassing for you that your younger, plainer sister should be the first to be engaged.'

A muscle twitched in Euphemia's cheek, but she was not to be defeated so easily. 'Ah, Orinda,' she replied, fanning herself gently, 'it may be I will have similar news soon, but if I do, I intend to announce it more discreetly.'

She cast an alluring glance at her dancing partner, who looked visibly startled by this hint. He was, however, enough of a gentleman not to question or contradict her, though there was an unpleasantly triumphant glint in his eye. Kate saw a cloud of uncertainty pass over Mrs Buckingham's features, but she rallied herself quickly and declared herself delighted at the prospect of having both her daughters engaged to be married.

'Now all we need to do is find a wealthy husband for you, Miss Spenser.'

'Indeed, madam, I would far rather work for my living and live up three pairs of stairs with a man I love, than wallow in luxury with one I do not.' As she uttered the words, Kate sensed Hawksley's eyes flicker towards her.

'Ah, you say that now, but if you were put to the test, my dear, it would be a different story.' Mrs Buckingham's melancholy smile made Kate realise in a blinding flash of insight that that was what had happened to her. 'You should have heard the plans your mother and I made when we were girls. In those days it was love or nothing.'

* * *

Throughout supper, Kate observed Euphemia as she exerted herself to be more charming than ever, smiling and laughing at the dullest of jokes, while Mr Watson gave hard stares and pointed remarks if she should so much as look at another man. Kate knew her friend's confidence in her ability to tame him. No man had failed to bend to Euphemia's will.

Apart from John Hawksley. Kate sensed it still irked Euphemia that she had not been able to find the one weakness that would have enabled her to break through his reserve — and that Frederick Clinton had engaged himself to her sister. By careful manoeuvring, Euphemia contrived to place herself alongside Frederick Clinton as they made their way back to the ballroom after supper and slipped her hand confidingly though his arm as she said, 'It will be so odd to have to think of you as a brother.'

'I am certain we will grow accustomed to it,' he replied in a cool tone.

'Oh, I daresay we will,' she agreed, smiling her most dreamy, seductive smile. 'After all,' she purred. 'We are such good friends already.'

Clinton clearly took her by surprise by gently but firmly extracting his arm from her grasp and turning to face her. 'For your sister's sake, I hope we can remain friends,' he said with uncharacteristic gravity. 'I love Orinda very much and therefore find it difficult to forgive anyone who makes her cry.'

Euphemia gasped aloud, for once speechless and unable to retort before he turned and walked away from her. As Euphemia clenched her fists unconsciously, Mr Watson's voice just behind them made her jump.

'Miss Buckingham . . . what did Clinton want with you?'

'Oh, I was just welcoming him to the family, no more than that,' she said, turning on her most radiant smile. 'Is that all you wished to say to me?'

'No, madam, I also think it's high time I should have an answer.'

'An answer? I do not believe you have yet asked me a question.'

Mr Watson's jaw tightened, but

Euphemia was clearly undaunted. 'Do not toy with me, madam. Do you or do you not intend to marry me?'

Thoughts of Sir Peter Harrington's title flitted across Euphemia's mind, but with her connections and his ambition, she knew Mr Watson could become a magistrate, a member of parliament, perhaps even a baronet, whereas Sir Peter would never achieve anything. She softened her features in an approximation of affection and flicked open her fan to hide the absence of a blush. 'Oh, sir, can it be you have doubted my feelings for a second?'

'Am I to take it that is an acceptance?'

Euphemia breathed a surreptitious sigh of relief and allowed her head to droop modestly. 'If it pleases you, sir.'

This meekness seemed to take the wind out of Mr Watson's sails. Euphemia hid her triumphant smile behind the fluttering of her fan. There was nothing she liked so much as to confound her numerous admirers. And she had no intention of giving them up after her marriage — though she knew it would be as well not to tell Mr Watson that just yet.

★ ★ ★

Kate paid the price for her incessant dancing the following day. Her old injury flared up to such an extent that she could not conceal her limp. Fortunately she was not expected to exert herself much, since the morning was to be spent receiving calls from their respective dancing partners. Kate found herself watching Mr Watson more attentively than she might have done if Mrs Buckingham had not confided in her after breakfast.

'I am sure he is perfectly respectable and I daresay Euphemia knows what she is doing,' she murmured with her usual distracted air, 'but Mr Buckingham is not best pleased with the match — he thinks she ought to have held out for someone with birth and breeding as well as wealth. But after all, the rumours that Mr Watson owns shares in a slaver might not be true and he is received in all the best houses, even though I cannot quite warm to his manner . . .'

It was so out of character for Mrs Buckingham to speak ill of anybody that Kate had hardly known what to say. 'Mr Watson is not, I suspect, the most easy-tempered of men,' she ventured.

'Easy-tempered. Yes, that's just the thing. Not at all like Mr Clinton. But I daresay Euphemia will manage somehow.' Her expression remained troubled, however, despite these attempts to reassure herself.

And so Kate found herself watching both betrothed couples. There was something endearing about the way Frederick Clinton and Orinda giggled and teased one another, like naughty children. Moreover, Clinton seemed utterly oblivious to Euphemia's attempts to lure him back into her orbit.

But observing the other couple made Kate shudder. Mr Watson bore Euphemia's tyranny patiently enough for the moment, but Kate formed the impression he was only biding his time, intending to show Euphemia who was her master as soon as the wedding ring should be on her finger. So concerned was Kate that she tried to voice her fears when she was alone with Euphemia before dinner. But Euphemia merely laughed. 'I never took you to be the type to be envious of another girl's good fortune.'

After that, it seemed wiser to hold her tongue and hope Euphemia would not live to regret her decision, because Kate was coming to the conclusion that an unhappy marriage was a far worse fate than remaining a spinster.

Her ankle was much better by the next morning, but she used it as an excuse not to accompany Mrs Buckingham and her daughters on a shopping expedition to Oxford Street. She felt she could not stand any more talk of weddings unless she had some respite first.

John Hawksley had not called the previous day, but then, she told herself, she had never expected him. Yet when she heard a rap at the front door, not fifteen minutes after the Buckinghams' departure, her heart leapt. But even when he was shown into the drawing room, she could scarcely believe he was really there. She barely heard the polite conversation that passed between Hawksley and her mother, until without warning Mrs Spenser rose and made some excuse about a task she had forgotten to carry out.

'So,' Hawksley said, 'how is your music coming along?'

Kate shook her head. 'There is hardly time for such things here,' she said, then could not resist adding, 'I am surprised at your concern. I formed the impression the other night that now you have such fine new friends, you did not intend to recognise us.'

'I am sorry I gave that impression. I had no such intention.'

Kate looked down at her hands and bit her lip. She had no idea how she should proceed. She was achingly aware of how close and how distant he was at one and the same time, and contradictory impulses tormented her.

'I would offer to resume teaching you, but — ' he paused to choose his words — 'given all that has occurred, I'm unsure that would be a good idea.'

'No,' Kate agreed, but she felt her heart break as she uttered the word.

There was another long silence. Hawksley stirred, as if about to rise, and Kate looked up sharply, terrified that she might never see him again — or, worse still, that she would see him frequently but be forced eternally to hide her feelings for him. But Hawksley had settled into his seat again.

'I apologise if I have offended you,' he said. 'I should prefer it if we could part as friends.'

It was another twist of the knife. She could not stay silent any longer. 'Friends?'

she echoed. 'Do you really think that is possible?' Hawksley flinched and it was another wrench at her heart. Desperation made Kate reckless. 'You had no right to kiss me like that and then abandon me without explanation.' Her voice quivered with suppressed tears.

'I sent you a letter. Did you not receive it?'

'Oh yes, your letter. Did it ever occur to you that my feelings on the matter might be as important as yours?'

He looked at her then, so intently that she found she could neither breathe nor look away. She saw understanding dawn in his eyes, as if he would not allow himself to believe he had interpreted her words correctly. 'Miss Spenser, I had believed you were engaged to Frederick Clinton.'

Her breath caught in her throat as she told him, 'I turned him down months ago at Fairfield.'

It was precisely at that moment that Kate's mother chose to return. Kate heard nothing of what followed. It seemed an agonisingly long time that he stayed, and yet far too soon when Hawksley announced he ought to be going. Mrs Spenser made some attempt to prolong his visit, but he merely shook his head. Kate was not sure how she managed to say farewell. The only thing that seemed real was the fierce grip of his hand, which caused her to look up into his eyes. And then he was gone.

Her mother escorted him out into the hall and Kate forced herself not to dash to the window for one last glimpse. Instead, blindly, she found her way to the piano and began to play his sonata so she would not hear the outer door closing behind him. She vaguely heard the drawing room door open and shut, but she went on playing. It could only be her mother.

Her eyes filled with tears, but it made no difference. Her fingers instinctively snatched the right notes, swooping from high up on the keyboard to the low, crashing last chord. She could not endure any more. She leaned her elbows on the narrow ledge next to the ivory keys and covered her face with both hands as she burst into violent sobs.

She heard a swift movement behind her, the low, gently cry. A pair of hands settled on her shoulders. 'Don't cry, Kate. Please don't cry.'

She gasped at the sound of his voice and twisted round. 'What are you doing here?' she asked, swiping at her cheeks.

'Your mother sent me. She thinks we still have things to say to each other.' His voice grew more and more hesitant with every word. 'She thinks that you return my love.'

At the same moment, his hands slid down her arms, encircling her as he pressed his lips to the nape of her neck. The sensation that darted through her made her gasp involuntarily. She clasped his hands, afraid he would misunderstand and pull away from her. Instead, he breathed her name and kissed her again and again, allowing his mouth to travel down her neck and shoulders. Kate lifted his hand in both of hers so she could kiss his palm and cradle it against her cheek.

He seemed to understand what she wanted to say. Keeping his arms around her, he changed his position so he was sitting on the edge of the stool facing her. Her hands ran up his broad chest, over his shoulders, twining around his neck.

'Marry me,' he murmured, his forehead pressed against hers. 'You'll have to work for a living, live in hired rooms, save to make ends meet . . . '

'What do such things matter when we are miserable when we are apart?'

He smiled roguishly. 'For that you deserve another kiss.'

It wasn't until she was breathless that he tucked her head against his shoulder, so he could rest his cheek against her hair and trace every contour of her ear. 'It must be soon,' he said softly. 'Otherwise I cannot answer for myself that I will be able to behave like a gentleman and not take advantage of you shamefully.'

Kate kissed the hollow at the base of his throat. 'I care not what you do or where we go,' she said, 'so long as you never to leave me behind again.'

He tipped her head back for another kiss. 'I promise, my love.'

THE END

We do hope that you have enjoyed reading this large print book.

Did you know that all of our titles are available for purchase?

We publish a wide range of high quality large print books including:
Romances, Mysteries, Classics
General Fiction
Non Fiction and Westerns

Special interest titles available in large print are:
The Little Oxford Dictionary
Music Book, Song Book
Hymn Book, Service Book

Also available from us courtesy of Oxford University Press:
Young Readers' Dictionary
(large print edition)
Young Readers' Thesaurus
(large print edition)

For further information or a free brochure, please contact us at:
Ulverscroft Large Print Books Ltd.,
The Green, Bradgate Road, Anstey,
Leicester, LE7 7FU, England.
Tel: (00 44) **0116 236 4325**
Fax: (00 44) **0116 234 0205**

LOVE AND CHANCE

Susan Sarapuk

When schoolteacher Megan bumps into a gorgeous Frenchman in the Hall of Mirrors at Versailles, she thinks she will never see him again. Until the Headteacher asks her to visit Lulu Santerre, a pupil who is threatening not to return to school. Megan discovers that Lulu's brother Raphael is the man she met at Versailles ... When Lulu goes missing Raphael and Megan are thrown together and both of them have to make decisions about their future.

WISH YOU WERE HERE?

Sheila Holroyd

Cara was hoping to spend Christmas in England with her boyfriend, but her mother sweeps her off to a holiday home in Spain. However, they are forced to stay in a hotel, wondering if they can afford the bill. There, she becomes attracted to Nick, despite his being ten years her junior. But, unexpectedly, her boyfriend, Geoff, and Nick's girlfriend, Lily, appear at the hotel. Then both Nick's and Cara's fathers add to the complicated network of relationships . . .

CLOSER!

Julia Douglas

Jess Watkins realises that she's a dreamer with no ambitions when her friend Becky gets married. However, she manages to land herself a job as secretary at the Brachan Window Company. Her boss, Jared King, makes a big impression on her — and not just professionally. But she finds that Jared is married to Suzanne. Then, her career begins to blossom, although the office seems in danger of closing. Working in a double-dealing world, can Jess ever find true love?